THE PERFECTION OF LOVE

Lord Rowley known as Roué Rowley is the most attractive raffish eccentric of his time. Alone exiled from England by the strictly converted society round Queen Victoria he is worried that his reputation will hurt his daughter. He arranges for Darcia to be chaperoned by the widow of the French Ambassador to the Court of St James and for his daughter to be legally the Countess de Sauze.

THE PERFECTION OF LOVE

The Perfection Of Love

by

Barbara Cartland

Magna Large Print Books
Long Preston, North Yorkshire,
BD23 4ND, England.

British Library Cataloguing in Publication Data.

Cartland, Barbara
    The perfection of love.

    A catalogue record of this book is
    available from the British Library

    ISBN   0-7505-2005-1

First published in Great Britain 1980

Copyright © Barbara Cartland 1980

Cover illustration by arrangement with Rupert Crew Ltd.

The moral right of the author has been asserted

Published in Large Print 2003 by arrangement with
Cartland Promotions, care of Rupert Crew Limited

Magna Large Print is an imprint of Library Magna Books Ltd.

Printed and bound in Great Britain by
T.J. (International) Ltd., Cornwall, PL28 8RW

AUTHOR'S NOTE

As a background for the novel I have described the building of Waddesdon Manor from 1874 to 1889 by Baron Ferdinand de Rothschild. He combined the beauty of the 16th century French Chateaux I have mentioned to create in England one of the most beautiful, exotic, fairy tale houses one can imagine.

The rooms and the furniture I have described can all be seen at Waddesdon which is open to the public with the exception of the picture of Venus, Mercury and Cupid by Louis Michel Van Loo.

Waddesdon has more treasures packed into its rooms than any other house I have ever visited and everyone who loves beautiful antiques which are historic should be grateful to James de Rothschild who on his death in 1957, bequeathed the house and its contents to the National Trust.

CHAPTER ONE

1882

'I understand, Darcia, that your aunt wishes you to visit her tomorrow in Paris.'

'Yes, Reverend Mother.'

'You know that I disapprove of my pupils going to Paris or having anything to do in the city?'

'Yes, Reverend Mother.'

'I should have thought that you might have explained this to your aunt and that instead she could have come to see you here in the Convent.'

'Perhaps, Reverend Mother, she would find the journey too arduous.'

There was silence as the Reverend Mother regarded the girl facing her the other side of the desk with scrutinising eyes.

There was no doubt that Darcia, since she had been in her charge, had blossomed into a beauty.

Perhaps it was this that made her feel reluctant, very reluctant, although she could not explain why, to allow the girl even strictly chaperoned to journey from the quiet cloistered atmosphere of the Convent School to what was spoken of all over Europe as 'The gayest City in the World'.

Nevertheless the Reverend Mother had to admit that Darcia had proved a model pupil in every way.

She had worked hard, in fact there was no other girl in the school who had achieved such academic distinction and although she was the only English pupil she had been liked by all those of other nationalities and undoubtedly was a favourite with the teaching Nuns.

She thought that Darcia's hair with red lights in it and her eyes of a strange hazel-green colour were unique even among the hundreds of girls who had passed through her hands.

She liked the way Darcia sat waiting to hear if she could visit her aunt without pleading her case or showing any impatience at the delay, although she had received neither a refusal nor an acceptance.

The Reverend Mother made up her mind.

'Very well, Darcia,' she said. 'You may go to Paris, and as your aunt has said she is sending a Courier for you that will certainly save me providing you with an escort. But you must make it clear that this kind of arrangement is not entirely to my satisfaction.'

'I will do that, Reverend Mother,' Darcia said quietly, 'and thank you very much for saying I can accept my aunt's invitation.'

'A messenger is waiting, so you must write a note immediately,' the Reverend Mother said.

'Thank you,' Darcia replied again and made a respectful curtsy before she went from the room.

Only as she shut the door of the study did she give a little skip for joy and ran with what the Mother Superior would have thought unseemly haste to her classroom which for the moment was empty.

She opened her desk, pulled out a leather-covered blotter in which there was some writing-paper and scribbled a few lines.

The Reverend Mother would in fact, have been extremely surprised if she had read what Darcia had written:

Dearest Dear:
I cannot wait for tomorrow and I will be with you as quickly as your horses can travel.
My love and a thousand kisses,
Darcia.'

She sealed the envelope, then moving demurely carried the note to the Hall where a Nun on duty took it from her to hand to the groom who was waiting for it outside.

He was riding, Darcia saw as she peeped through the half-open door, a well-bred and doubtless swift horse.

Then she ran upstairs to decide what she would wear tomorrow when she would visit Paris for the first time in two years.

The carriage that arrived for Darcia early the next morning was an extremely comfortable one, well-sprung but anonymous in that there was no crest or coat of arms painted on the panels of the doors, nor did the silver harness on the four horses carry any insignia.

There was a coachman and a footman on the box, and the Courier who waited respectfully outside the door of the Convent was an elderly man with white hair who bowed to Darcia when she appeared.

She inclined her head, but did not speak as she stepped into the carriage.

The elderly man seated himself with his back to the horses and as the carriage drove off Darcia bent forward to wave her hand to the Nun watching them drive away before she shut the Convent door.

Only then did Darcia lean back at her ease and say to the man opposite her:

'How are you, Briggy?'

'All the better for seeing you, Miss Darcia!' was the reply. 'You've grown and changed so much in the last two years that it's doubtful if the Master'll recognise you.'

'I am longing to see him!' Darcia said in a soft voice. 'It has been a very, very long two years without him.'

'I thought you'd feel that, Miss Darcia,' Mr Briggs replied. 'But the Master was determined you should be well educated.'

'I am so stuffed with knowledge,' Darcia replied, 'that I feel sometimes as if I was a pot of pâté de foie gras.'

They both laughed.

'How is Papa?'

'He's well,' Mr Briggs replied, 'but I don't have to tell you, Miss Darcia, he's still burning the candle at both ends.'

'Could he do anything else?' Darcia enquired. 'It would be strange if he did.'

'Strange indeed.'

'Where are you staying? I thought our house in Paris was shut up.'

'We've opened it, Miss Darcia, especially so that the Master can meet you there, and

I was to tell you that no-one's to see you or know you're visiting him, and that's important.'

Darcia looked surprised, but before she could speak Mr Briggs went on:

'The Master told me to give you this veil to put over your bonnet as you walk from the carriage into the house. He doesn't want the servants to know where you've come from and the coachman's been sworn to secrecy. As he's been with us for a long time he's not likely to talk.'

Darcia gave a little laugh of sheer amusement.

'This all sounds very like Papa, but why? What is the reason for such secrecy and the need for me to be invisible?'

'You'll certainly not be that, Miss Darcia,' Mr Briggs replied, 'and if you'll not think it impertinent of me to say so, you've grown so beautiful that the Master will be in for a big surprise.'

'I hope so, I hope so very much,' Darcia said. 'I have always known ever since I was a child that Papa only liked pretty women, and I used to pray every night that when I grew up I would be pretty enough to please him.'

'Your prayers have certainly been answered,

Miss Darcia.'

'Thank you, Briggy, that is exactly what I wanted to hear.'

Darcia had spoken truly when she said she had known all her life that her father liked pretty women and they liked, or rather the right word was 'loved', him.'

The only trouble was that they came and went with such rapidity that she had no sooner got used to some alluring charmer living in the house and obviously enjoying a very intimate relationship with her father than her place was taken by another, and yet another.

Looking back she often found it hard to remember their names or to distinguish their features one from another.

One thing they all had in common was that, because they wished to ingratiate themselves with the dashing, handsome, raffish Lord Rowley, they went out of their way to pet and spoil his only child.

Curiously this had no affect on Darcia's character.

Even when she was very young she realised that so much they said to her was insincere and that the affection they showed her was an act performed to impress her father.

She could understand their feelings

because to her there was no-one more attractive, more fascinating – perhaps the right word was 'mesmeric' than the man who was described by the world as the greatest roué of his time.

As she grew older Darcia realised with an intelligence far beyond her years that her father had been born in the wrong period.

In the wildly raffish Georgian days he would have been in his element, a leader of the Bucks and Beaux who circled round 'The Prince of Pleasure', the Prince Regent who was afterwards George IV.

Instead in the stifling propriety and respectability of Queen Victoria's Court Lord Rowley was considered an eccentric who went too far in his eccentricities, and in fact became one of the black sheep in a hypocritical society.

Not to be found out was the motto of those who managed to enjoy themselves without incurring the displeasure of 'The Widow of Windsor'.

This meant using a certain amount of caution, but Lord Rowley had never known what it was to be cautious. He flouted the conventions until England became too hot for him and he moved abroad, taking with him as a parting gesture one of the Queen's favourite Ladies-in-Waiting, who believed foolishly and erroneously that the Social World was well lost for love.

It was the uproar that followed this action which made Lord Rowley feel he must do something about his daughter.

A month before her sixteenth birthday Darcia was sent to the Convent de Sacré Coeur after an unusually extensive search on her father's part, to find a School where first there would be no other English girls, and secondly the standard of education was exceptionally high.

Darcia did not question his decision, having learned over the years that was a hopeless waste of time, but she was rather surprised when he told her that she had been admitted to the School under the name of 'Darcia Rowell'.

Before she could ask the obvious questions he explained with a twinkle in his eye:

'First, if they knew who your father was, I doubt if they would have accepted you, and secondly from now on, you have to be yourself and not be contaminated by your connection with me.'

'I am not contaminated, Papa,' Darcia replied angrily. 'I am proud, very, very proud to be your daughter. No other girl in the whole world could have such an exciting, original parent, or one who made life such fun.'

'That would be all right if you were a boy,' Lord Rowley replied, 'but you are a girl, my dear, and I hope, a very pretty one. That is why I have to give you a chance to be yourself, and this is the first step.'

He walked across the floor of the magnificent room in which they were talking before he added:

'When you are older I will explain more of the difficulties you will encounter, but for the moment I want you to grow up not only beautiful but clever, while most women are fools. That is why a man grows easily bored with them after a very short time.'

'I thought Dolores – I cannot remember her other name – who was with us – was it eight months ago? – had more brains than the rest,' Darcia said.

Her father laughed before he replied:

'She had another deficiency, but it is not something I should be discussing with you.'

'Why not, Papa?'

'Because, Dammit, you are my daughter and you are a lady.'

Her father's expression was serious as he said:

'I am going to send you away for two years.'

Darcia gave a cry of horror, and he added sharply:

'I am not going to argue about it. I am doing this for your sake and God knows I shall miss you! But I know it is right.'

There were no arguments after that, and young though she was, Darcia realised exactly what he wanted of her and set herself to satisfy him.

The majority of the women who had been in her father's life had been Ladies of Quality, and if there were others of a different type, as she had heard there were, he never brought them home.

The ladies were well born, many of them married to husbands of great social importance, who had been swept off their feet and excited by an irrepressible infatuation to behave both recklessly and foolishly.

Apart from that however, their example to Darcia was that of someone gently born, and she knew that her father would not tolerate bad manners or anything that he considered ungraceful in those around him.

At the Convent Darcia found there were a great many extra lessons of which she was sure her father would approve.

The girls did not only have special teachers in dancing and riding, but could also, if they wished, although surprisingly few did, learn fencing.

This was really frowned on by the Mother Superior but had been insisted on by some of the Italian parents who believed it gave their daughters some subtlety and the same quick reaction they required in their sons.

Besides this, Darcia became proficient at playing the piano, at singing and of course painting, although she insisted on being taught with oils rather than the watercolours that were considered more lady-like.

She applied herself to everything she could learn with single-minded concentration simply because she knew it was what her father wanted and she was determined to please him.

Lord Rowley might be a roué, but he was also an extremely intelligent man.

He spoke at least five languages perfectly, and he had surprisingly, though he had never had proper time to work, attained a degree at Oxford, and he was besides being an unsurpassed judge of a woman, also an expert on horseflesh.

He took up racing and won all the Classic

races and, because he had a flamboyant style which made him a favourite with the public, received louder cheers than any Royalty at every race-course at which he appeared.

He promoted his public image, again with Royal disapproval, by adopting the colour yellow and applying it to almost everything he owned.

The farm-carts on his estate, his Phaetons, his chaises and his travelling-carriages were all in yellow, and he himself was never seen without a yellow carnation in his buttonhole.

The crowds called him 'Rowley the Roué', and loved him.

His friends borrowed his money, made excuses for his outrageous behaviour, and were whole-heartedly loyal until the tide of disapproval made it, they felt, impossible for them to continue.

Only Lord Rowley's women never wavered, but loved him despairingly even after he discarded them.

As the carriage in which Darcia was travelling neared Paris she found her heart beating a little apprehensively in case after all the work she had done to please her father, after all the trouble she had taken with her appearance, he would be disappointed.

21

She had practised every movement she made, every gesture of her hands, to try and be as graceful as a ballerina.

She listened to her own voice singing and talking until she was convinced that it was musical.

She had not forgotten that her father had once said about some woman who was pursuing him:

'She has a voice like a corncrake! Women should sound like nightingales if one is expected to listen to them.'

She had also, and this had been really hard work, insisted on having German lessons besides French, Spanish and Italian.

She was now proficient in all these languages and the only thing of which she was not certain was if her English was as good as it should be.

As the carriage drove through the Bois she bent forward eagerly, then remembering that her father did not wish her to be seen, sat back again.

As they moved into the wide streets where there were many elegant and grand houses Mr Briggs without saying anything, held out the veil.

It was, Darcia thought with amusement, just the sort of veil her father would send her, not dark or ugly, but soft and delicate as a spider's web. Its colour was blue and it had tiny blue dots scattered over it which were a disguise in themselves.

She put it over her small bonnet and hanging to the edge of her shoulders it was in fact, both beguiling and intriguing.

She was wearing a gown she had bought but which had been far too elaborate to wear at School.

It had a larger bustle for one thing than the girls were permitted to wear, and the very tight bodice above her tiny waist revealed the perfection of her figure in a manner which would have been frowned on by the Mother Superior.

Darcia had seen the gown illustrated in a French magazine and had persuaded one of her friends to order it for her when she went home for the holidays.

'It will be very expensive from that particular dressmaker,' her friend had warned.

'That does not matter,' Darcia replied. 'I must have one gown that I would not be ashamed to wear if one of my relations invited me to visit them.'

'Are you hoping one will?' her friend enquired. 'They never come here, Darcia, and you never go home in the holidays.'

'My relations living in England,' Darcia replied, 'and they want me to finish my time at School before I join them.'

There were a few other girls who were in the same position.

One was Greek, another came from Teheran.

Darcia therefore did not spend the holidays alone, but she was always glad when the rest of the pupils returned and the ordinary School routine began again.

The carriage drew up at an impressive front door, and Darcia saw there were several liveried servants waiting.

There was a red carpet on the steps and as she walked into the house she had not seen for over five years, she thought it was so redolent of her father that she would have known it was his even if she had not been expecting to meet him there.

The pictures and the magnificent furniture were all part of his background in every house he owned. So too were the huge arrangements of flowers that decorated the Hall and which scented the Salon into which she was shown.

But Darcia for the moment was not concerned with anything but the man who was standing at the far end of the room.

Throwing back her veil with a little cry of sheer joy she ran towards him.

'Papa! Oh, Papa, how wonderful to see you!'

It was difficult to say the words, and yet they seemed to burst from her lips and her voice lilted with sheer joy as she spoke them.

Lord Rowley caught her in his arms and kissed her on both cheeks before he said:

'It has been a long time, my poppet. Let me look at you.'

He held her at arms' length, and as if she felt a little shy at this scrutiny Darcia undid the ribbons of her bonnet and threw it on the floor before she moved closer to him to kiss him again and again.

'You are lovely!' Lord Rowley said with satisfaction, 'and very much like your mother when I first saw her. She was fairer than you, but you have her features and I thought when you grew up you would be a beauty. I have backed the right horse again.'

Darcia laughed.

'Oh, Papa, I cannot tell you how marvellous it is to hear your voice and listen to the funny way you always say things! But I am not a horse, I am a grown woman, and now can I come back and live with you?'

She knew this was the question she had

been longing to ask, and which had been in her mind from the very moment she received the letter which had accompanied the one to the Mother Superior saying that her 'aunt' wished to see her.

She had known immediately who it was from, not only because she had no aunt who would be interested in her, but also because in a corner of the writing-paper there was the secret sign that they had agreed on two years ago.

In her father's case it was a very small 'R' and Darcia, because she said it was appropriate, drew him a tiny heart.

'That is what I have come to Paris to talk to you about,' Lord Rowley said now. 'But first tell me about yourself.'

'You know I have nothing to tell you, Papa, and I wrote everything that occurred in those incredibly boring letters that I inscribed every Sunday to my 'Uncle Rudolph', and sent to your Solicitors' office in London.'

Lord Rowley laughed.

'I must admit I found them hard reading, except for the ones you smuggled to me.'

'I could only do that when one of the girls I could trust was taken out by her relatives, or was going home for the holidays. Otherwise the Nuns scrutinised our letters to see if they were well written, and we were not making any complaints.'

'Did you have any?'

'No,' Darcia replied. 'It is exactly the sort of School of which you would approve! We are made to work, and our eternal souls are a constant concern!'

Lord Rowley was laughing as a servant came into the room carrying a bottle of champagne.

'I think,' Lord Rowley said, 'we should drink a toast to our reunion even though it will be a short one.'

'A short one, Papa?'

Lord Rowley did not reply but waited until the servant had left the room. Then he said:

'I have come over from Tangier especially to make arrangements for your future.'

'Is that where you have been? I wondered where you were living.'

'I have been there all the winter,' Lord Rowley said, 'but now it is getting warmer I am thinking of going to Greece.'

'Oh, Papa, let me come with you,' Darcia pleaded. 'I have been learning a little Greek and it would be very good for my education.'

'Your education as far as book-learning is

concerned should be complete by now.'

'Very well then, let me come because I want to be with you. I love you, Papa, and I have been counting the months, the days, the seconds, until we could be together again.'

There was a softness in Lord Rowley's eyes that few women evoked.

At fifty he still looked ten years younger, and he was in fact, extremely handsome, but it was not only that which made him so attractive.

It was the buccaneering glint in his eye, a slightly sardonic twist to his lips, and a kind of 'devil-may-care' attitude to life that gave him the power of a Pied Piper.

He took a sip of his champagne before he said:

'I have no wish to upset you, dearest child, but my plans are very different from yours, and although perhaps you will find it hard to believe, I am thinking of you and not of myself.'

Darcia looked at him anxiously. Then she said in a very small voice:

'Are you saying that you do not ... want me, Papa? I am nearly eighteen, and I cannot stay at School any longer.'

'I am well aware of that,' Lord Rowley

replied, 'and far from saying that I do not want you with me, I would like it more than anything else I can imagine. But at the moment I have to think of you.'

'Thinking of me would be to let me be happy, and you know whatever you are doing I would not interfere. I never got in your way in the past.'

'You were a child then,' Lord Rowley remarked. 'Now listen to me, Darcia, because it is important.'

He sat down on the sofa beside her and she knew that he was choosing his words carefully before he began:

'I loved your mother more than I have loved anyone in the whole of my life. She was not only the most beautiful person I have ever known, she was also the most intelligent.'

His voice was cynical as he went on:

'If she had lived, "Rowley the Roué" would never have existed. But she died and I have never allowed anyone to take her place.'

'Is that why you never re-married, Papa?' Darcia asked almost beneath her breath.

'That,' Lord Rowley agreed, 'and the fact that I have never found anyone like your mother with the exception of you.'

'I am glad I am like her.'

'Because you are like her and because I love you,' Lord Rowley went on, 'I have to give you the type of future she would want you to have.'

'Mama loved you, and therefore she would want me to be with you,' Darcia said quickly.

Her father shook his head, and she felt her spirits droop.

She had been certain on the way to Paris that this was the beginning of the life she had longed for, a life full of colour and excitement, fun and laughter, which her father had given her when she was a child.

'Now, what I have arranged,' Lord Rowley said in a different tone of voice, 'so that you will not be connected in any way with me, is that you will have a new identity, and make your way in the world to which you belong, without being handicapped by the stigma of being my daughter.'

'I do not consider it a stigma!' Darcia said angrily.

'My dear child,' Lord Rowley replied, 'I am not a fool. I know exactly what people think of me, and while it amuses me and I swear to you it does not trouble me in the slightest, I know exactly how it could destroy your chances and hurt you in a thousand ways, which I cannot bear to think about.'

'Then do not think about them,' Darcia begged. 'I shall not be hurt, Papa. I know what people have said about you, but I believe they are really envious, because you do what you want to do, and your friends would, I know, be kind to me, as they were when I was a little girl.'

'My friends would be kind to you,' Lord Rowley agreed, 'but because you are my daughter the doors of the houses to which I wish you to be invited and which should be open to you by birth would be closed.'

'They are not important.'

Lord Rowley shook his head.

'They are the houses where your mother was accepted and they are yours by right, provided you are not connected with "Rowley the Roué". As you know, the "sins of the fathers are visited upon the children unto the third and fourth generation".'

His voice was so serious that Darcia did not argue any more. She merely asked:

'What are you saying you want me to do, Papa?'

'I have been planning your future for a long time,' Lord Rowley replied. 'When you

31

leave School at the end of the term in three weeks' time, you will come to meet the *Marquise* de Beaulac in her house here in Paris.'

'Who is she?' Darcia asked.

She was very pale because what her father had said to her was a shock, but she had complete control over herself and her voice as she asked the question was calm.

'The *Marquise* de Beaulac,' Lord Rowley replied, 'is someone who you can trust, and who will be the only person you will meet in your new life who is aware of your real identity.'

He paused as if waiting for Darcia to say something, but when she remained silent he went on:

'The *Marquise* is a very old friend of mine. She is also the widow of a former Ambassador of France at the Court of St James's. She knows everyone of importance in London, and I can think of no-one better to introduce you as a debutante to English Society.'

'I presume,' Darcia said with just a slight edge on her voice, 'that the *Marquise* has a good reason for undertaking this task?'

Lord Rowley smiled.

'Our minds run on the same lines,' he

said, 'and there is no need for me to tell you the late Ambassador was a very extravagant man.'

'That is what I imagined the explanation would be,' Darcia said. 'Go on, Papa.'

'I have been wondering for a long time as to how I could make you sound important without using your own title, especially as I want you to make your debut in England.'

'And what have you decided?'

'I had the opportunity a year ago of buying from a Frenchman who was in difficulties, a very small island he owned off the West Coast of France. On the map it is little larger than a pin's head, but the ownership of the island of Sauze has carried with it the title of the *Comte* de Sauze accorded to a previous owner by the Holy Roman Empire over five hundred years ago.'

Lord Rowley saw by the look in Darcia's face that she was aware of how her father's story would end.

'You will therefore,' he said, 'become the *Comtesse* de Sauze, and I can assure you there will be no embarrassment on that score. The *Comte* who was the last of his family and a man over seventy when I met him, died two months ago.'

'That was certainly convenient for you,

Papa,' Darcia said, and her voice was sarcastic.

'I have always been lucky,' Lord Rowley said simply, 'and it is only what I had hoped might happen before you would need to use the title.'

'So now I am to be a Frenchwoman.'

'Only partially,' Lord Rowley said. 'To the world your father was half-French, your mother English, and I have procured quite a respectable-looking family tree for you, showing that the Graysons, a family that appears to have ceased to exist since the middle of this century, date back to the reign of Charles II.'

Lord Rowley paused before he added:

'I thought, seeing that you had my blood in you, that a touch of the "Merry Monarch" was most appropriate.'

For a moment Darcia, because she was resenting everything he was telling her, tried to resist the smile on his lips and the twinkle in his eyes.

Then suddenly she was laughing.

'Oh, Papa, you are incorrigible! How can you have dreamt up anything so fantastic, so utterly incredible?'

'On the contrary I think it will be very simple,' Lord Rowley said. 'I have tried to see every flaw and hole in my plan, and I swear to you that anyone would have to be a magician to untangle such a maze.'

Darcia was still laughing.

'The whole thing is ridiculous, and yet at the same time I am touched, very touched, Papa, that you are thinking of me.'

She made a little gesture with her hands.

'The trouble is I have no wish to be a smart debutante, to make my curtsy to the Queen as I am sure you are planning – or to move in what is usually known as "the Best Circles". I just want to be with you.'

She smiled as she went on:

'I can think of nothing more wonderful than to hear you saying: "I am fed up with this place! We will move on tomorrow morning," and the whole household begins to pack not knowing what their destination will be: a caravan across the Sahara, or a Piazza in Venice.'

'Stop tempting me,' Lord Rowley said. 'Like all women you always want the apple that is out of reach. No, my dear, one day, although you do not think so now, you will thank me because for the first time, I admit, I am behaving as your father should.'

'You are not protecting me, you are making me miserable!' Darcia declared.

'Oh, Papa, we have had such fun together, and I do love you!'

'It is because I love you that you are damned well going to do what I tell you!' Lord Rowley said.

He spoke so forcefully that Darcia knew he was, in fact very tempted, to give in to her.

She had always known she could play a part in his life that no other woman could, and be closer to his heart, the real heart, which they never found.

Then as she hesitated wondering if she should put her arms round his neck and plead with him or reason it out logically and intelligently, he drew her to her feet and to her surprise took her to the side of the Salon where there was a huge gilt-framed mirror.

They stood in front of it and she could not help thinking how attractive they both looked.

She was very small beside him, and yet in a way there was some vague resemblance that was inescapable.

In her it was more spiritual and there was something very young, untouched and innocent about her face that was certainly not to be seen in Lord Rowley's handsome, mocking countenance. Then he said quietly:

'Look at yourself. You are beautiful, Darcia, and that is why it would be a crime I am not prepared to commit to allow you to waste such beauty living my sort of life, which is wrong, utterly wrong for you.'

'And if I do not think so…?' Darcia began.

He stopped her by putting his finger to her lips.

'Because you love me,' he said, 'you will do what I want you to do, and because I love you I shall cut you out of my life, at least until the time you need me for a very different reason from what you are suggesting now.'

She understood what he meant and gave a deep sigh.

'Must I … really do … this, Papa?'

'You will do it because I loved your mother and because I love you and because, although we pretend otherwise, we both know right from wrong,' Lord Rowley said.

For a moment their eyes met in the mirror in front of them, and Darcia knew that she was fighting a silent battle.

Then inevitably her father won, and she thought bitterly she must surrender.

She did not have to speak; he knew instinctively that she had laid down her arms and he was the victor.

He put his hand round her shoulders.

'Now for the rest of this evening,' he said in a very different voice, 'let us enjoy ourselves, wildly, madly and quite irrepressibly, until it is time for you to return to the Convent.'

CHAPTER TWO

As the train drew into Victoria Station Darcia knew that this was the beginning of a new life.

It had already started when she was in Paris, but with the *Marquise* she did not have to pretend that she was not her father's daughter, or that they were not both of them embarking on a strange adventure which could only have been conceived in his facile mind.

The *Marquise* was everything that Darcia expected.

She had been very beautiful in her youth and was still lovely, despite her first grey hairs and a few inescapable wrinkles around her expressive dark eyes.

As soon as they talked together Darcia realised that the *Marquise* had not only a quick intelligence but also a sense of humour.

On her way to Paris from the Convent she had been a little apprehensive in case her father was settling her once again in a dull, conventional atmosphere such as she had known for the last two years.

After the gaiety and unpredictability of the life she had lived with him, at times she had found it unbearable.

She felt that having for two years done exactly what he had expected of her she should not have to do more.

There had however been a touch of laughter in the *Marquise* de Beaulac's eyes when she had asked after they had talked conventionally for a few minutes:

'Who but your father would have thought of anything so amusing, and at the same time incredible, as what we have to do?'

'That is exactly what I said to him,' Darcia replied.

'I have known your father for many years and he was a wonderful friend to my husband, and to – me.'

There was a note in the *Marquise's* voice which told Darcia what she had already guessed, that their relationship had been more than just friendship.

'It is not only that I wish to do what he wants where you are concerned,' the *Marquise* continued, 'but also his proposition, if that is the right word for it, has come at a moment in my life when I was feeling very sad, very depressed, feeling that in the world where I had played so interesting a part with my husband, there was now no place for me.'

'So we will both benefit through Papa's intrigue,' Darcia said, and liked the smile that lit up the *Marquise's* face.

Although she always had a little ache in her heart because she knew she would rather be with her father than with anyone else, she had been thrilled to shop in Paris, knowing she could spend as much as she wished on the beautiful, original gowns that she was well aware had made every woman who saw them envious.

She needed not only gowns but a whole wardrobe, and their shopping took time, while there was an endless procession of dress-boxes arriving at the *Marquise's* house.

But on Lord Rowley's instructions they were not allowed to linger in Paris.

'I want you to arrive in London at exactly the right moment,' he instructed his daughter. 'That is when the first batch of debutantes are no longer a novelty and the restless, bored social world will be looking for someone else to talk about.'

'And you intend that to be me?'

'I most certainly do, and to make sure you are, my dearest, I have rented the largest and most impressive house in Park Lane and bought you some superlative horses which will certainly attract the eyes of the men if your face fails to do so.'

He spoke as if that was an impossibility, but Darcia laughed and said:

'You have always said it was wise to "hedge your bets," Papa.'

'I am sure there is no need where you are concerned,' Lord Rowley replied, 'but you know without my saying so that, while a pretty face is a good introduction, it is important to have a few other tricks up one's sleeve.'

'What else have you planned for me?'

'A Ball after you have been presented to the Queen, and most stringent instructions to your chaperon to keep away the fortune-hunters, and the men like myself who are known as having a "roving eye".'

'I am beginning to think,' Darcia said teasingly, 'that the whole operation will be very expensive and very dull and, whatever your hopes, I shall remain a spinster.'

To her surprise her father did not laugh, instead his face was serious as he said:

'While it makes me jealous to think of you belonging to any other man, I know, my poppet, that you need a husband to look after you.'

'Only if I love him,' Darcia flashed.

'Love can come after marriage,' Lord Rowley said tentatively.

'So can boredom, dislike and aversion.'

Her father threw up his hands in a gesture that was more French than English.

'In which case,' he said, 'be careful when you fall in love!'

'I will be,' Darcia promised. 'But, Papa, however advantageous an alliance might be I have already sworn that I would never marry unless I was in love.'

'Then I can only hope,' her father replied, 'that your luck is as good as mine was.'

Sitting in the train running from Paris to Calais, Darcia put a question to the *Marquise* that had been in her mind for several days.

She had in fact been choosing her moment carefully and had waited until she thought she and her chaperon were so friendly, so compatible one to the other, that the *Marquise* would not attach any particular significance to the conversation.

'I have been trying to remember,' Darcia said, 'who I have met in London, and although I am certain they will not remember me, it will be interesting to see how they have

43

altered with the years.'

The *Marquise* looked a little worried.

'Your father is quite certain that none of his friends would recognise you.'

'I am sure Papa is right,' Darcia replied. 'I was thirteen when I was last in London and then it was only for a few nights. Before that we spent at least part of the year at Rowley Park and I loved every minute of it.'

The *Marquise* sighed.

'*Hélas!* I cannot bear to think of that beautiful house shut up.'

'Nor can I,' Darcia agreed, 'and perhaps one day when the gossip about Papa has died down and he is behaving with more propriety, he will be able to go back.'

The *Marquise* gave a little laugh.

'By that time your father will be in his dotage and walking on two sticks!'

'This is what I am afraid of,' Darcia said, 'but I want to go and look at my old home, even though it will make me unhappy.'

'You will have too much to think about, *ma chère* and to occupy you when you first arrive,' the *Marquise* said. 'But you were talking about the people you knew in England. Do you remember any of their names?'

Darcia thought.

'I remember one party in the country – it must have been for a Steeple-chase because I seem to recall that most of the men were Papa's hard-riding friends.'

As she spoke she was thinking back to an evening in the autumn.

She must have been about ten at the time and her Governess had put her to bed, but she would not go to sleep because her father had not come to kiss her goodnight.

She waited, then because she thought he had forgotten her she decided to go to him.

She slipped out of bed, put on her dressing-gown of white satin trimmed with little frills of lace, and moving on tip-toe so that no-one would hear her she went down the stairs to find her father.

She was aware as she reached the Great Hall that the ladies had already withdrawn from the Dining-Room and she could hear them talking in the Salon.

This meant that the gentlemen would be still drinking their port, and Darcia had run along a wide corridor which led to the magnificent Dining-Room hung with pictures of Rowley ancestors.

She had opened the Dining-Room door and seen as she expected that the gentlemen had all moved up the table to be near her father who was seated at the head of it.

Darcia could recall that they were laughing at something he had said, and he with a smile on his lips, looked so handsome and attractive that she felt her love for him move like a warm wave through her body.

She walked a little way into the room and her father saw her.

'Darcia!' he exclaimed in surprise, and she ran towards him.

'You never came to kiss me goodnight, Papa,' she said, 'so I had to come to you.'

'It was very remiss of me,' Lord Rowley said, 'and it will not happen again, my poppet.'

He picked her up as he spoke and sat her on his knee. One of the gentlemen at the table said:

'Whatever their age, Rowley, they all crave your kisses.'

'In a few years,' Lord Rowley replied, 'my daughter will not need to go in search of kisses from me or any other man.'

'That is true enough,' a gentleman said, 'and what could you expect her to be but a beauty?'

'Did you hear that, Darcia?' Lord Rowley had asked. 'These gentlemen say that you will be a beauty when you grow up. But remember, such compliments are seldom given unless they want something from you in return!'

'I protest,' one of the men sitting round the table cried, 'you are trying to turn the child into a cynic! Leave her with her illusions until she is at least as old as we are.'

'She would do better to develop her judgement and learn to assess both a man and a horse at their true worth,' Lord Rowley replied.

Darcia who had been looking at the table with its glittering lights and shining gold ornaments, was now attentive to the last remark.

'Sam says I am a very good judge of horseflesh like you, Papa,' she said, 'but why should I want to judge men?'

There was a burst of laughter at this and because Darcia was not certain whether they were laughing at her or at what she had said, she looked puzzled.

She then saw sitting at the table amongst the older men a young man who she was certain she had never seen with her father before.

She wondered who he was, thinking that because he was not laughing like the rest but looking at her with quite a serious expression on his face, she rather liked him.

'I think it is time you went to bed, my dearest,' her father said. 'I will kiss you goodnight, and although these gentlemen would like to kiss you too, I suggest you merely curtsy to them and run back upstairs before anybody realises you have gone.'

He bent and kissed her cheek as he spoke and because she loved him Darcia flung her arms around his neck to hug him as she kissed him in return.

Then Lord Rowley put her down on the floor beside his chair.

She curtsied as he had told her to do and said a little shyly:

'Good ... night.'

'Goodnight,' several gentlemen replied, and one added: 'Keep me several dances at your first Ball.'

Darcia felt he did not expect an answer and with a last glance at her father she moved away towards the door.

Before she could reach it the young man whom she had noticed at the table rose to open it for her.

She looked up at him and smiled.

'Thank you very much.'

'Goodnight, happy dreams,' he replied.

She did not have to ask the following day

who the young man was, even though she had been thinking about him.

She heard her father talking in the stables and she knew almost instinctively to whom he was referring.

'The Earl of Kirkhampton's boy rides better than I anticipated anyone of his age would do,' he was saying.

He was speaking to Sam who had always looked after her father's horses and had taught her to ride when she was so small she could hardly walk.

'So Oi've always heard, M'Lord,' Sam replied, 'an' when Oi seed him riding in the Steeple-chase Oi knows the tales about him weren't no exaggeration.'

'They were not,' Lord Rowley confirmed. 'I would be proud of a son of mine who took hedges in such style.'

There was just a touch of bitterness in his voice, and Darcia had known instinctively that while he loved her he often wished she had been a boy.

'I will ride so well, Papa, that you will be just as proud of me,' she had said.

Her father had laughed and picked her up in his arms to seat her on the saddle of the horse she was to ride.

'I am proud of everything you do,' he said,

'so there is no need for you or me to be jealous of any young man.'

As the years passed Darcia had often heard her father and his friends talk of the Earl of Kirkhampton's son and his amazing prowess in the field of sport.

Then she had seen him again when one night her father had had a party in London.

She had known by the embarrassed expression on her Governess's face and the way when she asked about the party every excuse was made not to give her a direct answer that it would be the type of hospitality which gave her father a bad name.

She had grown used to not asking questions but learning what she wished to know by overhearing his conversations with his friends.

It was not difficult for Darcia to guess that the ladies who were to be entertained were of the theatrical profession.

Actresses were considered very fast, she was aware of that, but from what the servants said she learnt that her father was interested in the well-known actress then performing at Drury Lane and the party was in her honour.

'I wish I could see the guests,' Darcia said

to herself.

She knew that even to suggest such an idea to her Governess would be to find herself locked in her bedroom.

Nevertheless she was determined not to be left out of what she was sure her father would find a very enjoyable evening.

All day the preparations went on downstairs. There was to be a supper-party after the theatres closed, then dancing in one of the big rooms and gaming in another.

Darcia was aware that the green-baize tables were being set out and great mountains of flowers were being brought into the house.

Her father was fond of flowers, and wherever he was they were arranged in every room and scented the air in a manner that Darcia felt increased the fairy-tale aura around him.

Evading her Governess, she managed after a frustrating day of not being able to see him to slip into his bedroom when he was dressing for the evening.

As always he was pleased to see her and she thought as he stood in his shirt-sleeves brushing his hair with two ivory brushes in front of a gilt mirror that he looked very handsome.

'I would like to come to your party tonight, Papa.'

'I am sure you would, my precious,' he replied, 'but it is the sort of party that you cannot attend now, nor even when you are grown up.'

'Why not?'

'Because, my poppet, you were born what is called a "Lady".'

Darcia had expected this answer and she made a little grimace.

'It is a pity I am not a gentleman.'

'A great pity,' her father agreed, 'but there is nothing you can do about it, and much as I would like you with me this is the sort of evening when you are in one world and I am in another.'

Darcia had sat down on his bed.

'If I dressed up as a boy could I come?'

Her father had laughed and turned to look at her.

'With your eyes and your skin. I doubt if you could deceive a blind man!'

He turned back to the dressing-table saying:

'Actually there will be only men of my age at my party, with the exception of Kirkhampton's son.'

'Why have you asked him, Papa?'

'Because he rode a remarkable race and won it yesterday, and I thought he deserved a little fun after all the training he must have done to get himself down to the right weight.'

'You like him, do you not, Papa?'

'Very much,' Lord Rowley replied. 'He is a very outstanding rider, but he takes life a little too seriously. Perhaps I will be able to cheer him up.'

He was talking as he often did, as though he was speaking to one of his contemporaries, and Darcia said:

'If he pleases you I would like to meet him.'

'There is plenty of time for that when you are older.'

The Valet was waiting to help Lord Rowley into his tight-fitting long-tailed evening coat, but before he did so, he picked up Darcia in his arms and kissed her.

'Go to bed, my precious,' he said, 'and in seven years time I will produce all the best-looking, most eligible and finest riders in the country for your approval.'

'I only want to be with you, Papa,' Darcia had answered.

'By that time you will think I am far too old,' her father answered.

She knew, however, as he kissed her again, that he had been pleased at what she had said.

Because the idea of the man her father admired kept returning to her mind she was determined to see him again, and she had an opportunity quite unexpectedly when she was riding in the Park with Sam.

Her father was away for the day and instead of riding with him as she often did when he was in London, Sam had escorted her, and after they had galloped in the unfashionable part of Hyde Park, they had ridden down Rotten Row.

Darcia had always been entranced by the elegance of the ladies in their skin-tight habits riding horses as fine as any her father owned, and escorted by gentlemen who did not ride as well as he did.

Then coming towards them she saw a superlative rider, a man who seemed a part of his horse and who had the kind of elegant expertise that proclaimed itself at the very first glance, but which she had never seen before except when she watched her father.

He drew nearer and without having to ask Sam who he was Darcia had recognised the young man who had opened the door for her at Rowley Park several years earlier.

She had known by the way heads turned in his direction that all those who were walking at the side of the road had noticed him as had those who were on horseback.

He paid no attention, passing by without smiling or raising his hat, and disappeared in the distance in the same sudden way that he had first appeared.

'You know who that is,' Darcia said to Sam.

'Aye, that be the young Earl o'Kirkhampton. Been buyin' a lot more horses he has, since he comes into the title. That be one o' the new ones he be tryin' out now.'

Darcia did not answer.

She was thinking of the way the Earl rode and found it easy to understand when she saw him that her father wished that she was a boy.

Now, thinking of him she deliberately did not immediately mention his name to the *Marquise*.

Instead she asked what had happened to an elderly man she remembered often being at Rowley Park.

'Lord Fitzherbert?' the *Marquise* replied. 'He died last year. So sad. My husband and I were very fond of him.'

'And Lord Arrington? I remember he was

a close friend of Papa's.'

'When I was last in England he had retired to his country-house suffering from gout. He too is getting on in years. I often think he was one of the wittiest men we ever entertained at the Embassy.'

'I can recall a younger man. I think his name was the Earl of Kirkhampton.'

Darcia hoped that her voice sounded quite natural but the *Marquise* exclaimed:

'Ah! My Lord Kirkhampton! I always thought he was exceedingly handsome, and of course one year nobody talked of anything but the races he won riding his own horses.'

There was silence, and then as the *Marquise* appeared to be looking back into the past Darcia said:

'Is he still winning races?'

'No, he still has horses, but he occupies his time with something very different.'

'What is that?'

'He has started to build a house.'

'Build a house!' Darcia exclaimed.

'Yes, his family mansion was burned down in a fire, and as it was in rather an inaccessible part of the country the Earl decided to build a new house on an estate he bought nearer to London.'

'It sounds a strange thing to do.'

Darcia was thinking as she spoke that nearly all her father's friends had ancestral houses like Rowley Park which had been passed down through five generations before it was inherited by her father.

Then she told herself there was really no reason for her surprise.

A great number of fine houses had been built in the 18th century and at the beginning of this one.

'It would be interesting,' the *Marquise* said, 'to know what type of house the Earl will build. When I left London he was so preoccupied with his new interest that he had been to no parties and his friends were complaining that they never saw him.'

'Where is this house he is building?' Darcia asked.

'Strangely enough it is not far from Rowley Park,' the *Marquise* replied. 'I remember thinking when I heard about it that your father might be resentful at having a near neighbour who would compete with his stable.'

Darcia did not reply. She was thinking that because it was the Earl of Kirkhampton her father would not have minded the competition as much as if it had been anybody else.

She, on the other hand, might have found it irritating to know that every time the Earl had a success on the Turf it made her father wish once again that she was his son rather than his daughter.

She had now found out all she wished to know and she therefore changed the subject.

Although she would never have mentioned it to the *Marquise* or to anybody else, she knew that she wanted to see the young man who was such a magnificent rider again.

The house in London was everything that Darcia had expected.

It was even larger than her father's and she thought that with its boarded-up windows Rowley House looked at her with reproachful eyes as she drove past it.

As soon as they arrived the *Marquise* contrived that they had a dozen invitations every day and the gowns Darcia had purchased in Paris caused a sensation.

Because the *Marquise* had last been in London as the wife of the French Ambassador with all the privilege of the Diplomatic Corps behind her, she was, even as a widow, of too great importance for anybody to ignore her.

But accompanied by an outstandingly

beautiful young girl who it was whispered was a great heiress there was no doubt that they quickly aroused the curiosity of the social world.

This made it imperative that they should be invited by every hostess who wished whatever entertainment she was planning to be a success.

Darcia found herself complimented and fêted and pursued by men of every age and each morning when she came downstairs it was to find the Hall filled with floral tributes from a whole host of new admirers.

'You are certainly a success, my dear!' the *Marquise* said as they inspected the cards.

The secretary made a list so that Darcia could write polite letters of thanks which gained her a reputation for having good manners as well as beauty.

The secretary who helped her had been provided by Lord Rowley.

Her father had told her that Briggs had chosen somebody she could trust with her finances as well as all her other arrangements.

'Curtis has actually been in my employment for some years,' Lord Rowley had said. 'You can give him any order, however extraordinary, and he will carry it out punctiliously. What is more, he has an ear to the ground.'

'What do you mean by that, Papa?'

'I mean,' Lord Rowley explained, 'that if you want to find out what is being said about yourself or anyone else, if you fancy that a man is only making up to you because he is heavily in debt, Curtis can find out the truth.'

'A spy, Papa?'

'Only when it is in your best interests,' Lord Rowley answered. 'Otherwise he will pay your bills, write your letters, run the household, and make sure you have everything you desire.'

'In which case he is a magician!' Darcia laughed.

She found on arrival in London that Curtis was a quiet, serious-looking man who always looked as if he had not slept well. His efficiency was astonishing and his organisation faultless.

The *Marquise* was quite prepared to leave all the planning of the household to him.

'I have a list of all the guests I think you will wish to invite, *Madame*,' Curtis said to the *Marquise*, 'and of course there may be additional names you wish to give me.'

Darcia looked quickly down the list.

It was in alphabetical order, and it was not hard to see that the Earl of Kirkhampton was not included.

She turned over several other pages.

'I think you have listed the whole of Debrett,' she said with a smile.

It was only when the *Marquise* had gone upstairs to rest that Darcia sought out Mr Curtis to speak to him alone in the small room he used as an office.

He rose as she entered and she thought there was a slight expression of surprise in his tired eyes.

'Sit down, Mr Curtis,' Darcia said. 'I just wanted to go through the list with you again of those asked to my Ball.'

Mr Curtis handed her the list and she sat down in a chair by the desk.

'I do not see the Earl of Kirkhampton,' she said without prevarication.

'I knew it would be useless to ask him, *Mademoiselle*.'

Mr Curtis was always very careful to remember her assumed rank and nationality even when they were alone.

'Why is that?' Darcia enquired.

'Because it is well known that the Earl has accepted no invitations for the past year.'

'Because he is building his house?'

'That is what I understand.'

'Tell me about him. He was a friend of my father's and I wish to know what he is doing and why.'

'I would like to check on everything I have heard about him before I report to you, *Mademoiselle*,' Mr Curtis replied.

'I would like to hear it now,' Darcia said.

There was an imperious note in her voice, and although she was not aware of it she reminded Mr Curtis of her father.

'Very well,' he replied. 'I am told, but I would like to verify it, that the Earl is building a house for the Lady Caroline Blakeley.'

There was a moment's silence before Darcia asked:

'You mean he intends to marry her?'

'It is said they are unofficially engaged, *Mademoiselle*.'

Again there was an obvious silence before Darcia said:

'I wish to see this building and in order to do so, I require a carriage that is not conspicuous to take me there.'

Mr Curtis nodded and she went on:

'I understand the site is not far from Rowley Park?'

'That is true, *Mademoiselle*, and it is in fact

near the village of Letty Green.'

For a moment Darcia looked as if the name meant nothing to her. Then she gave an exclamation.

'Letty Green!' she cried. 'That is where Miss Greythorn lives in a house that my father gave her when she retired from teaching me.'

'That was before my time, *Mademoiselle*,' Mr Curtis replied, 'but I will find out all particulars for you by tomorrow morning.'

'Do that,' Darcia ordered, and went from the room.

That night, after she had danced with many of the most eligible bachelors in London she found herself still thinking of the Earl of Kirkhampton who preferred building to dancing.

It seemed a strange occupation and very different from what she had suspected. If he had been training his horses, planning out a race-course, or even just concerned with new stables, it would have seemed somehow more in character.

But to be occupied in building a house for someone he intended to marry was different.

She had however already seen Lady Caroline Blakeley.

She had been certain that she would be at

the Ball for it was one of the largest of the Season and given by one of the hostesses whose invitations were as sought after as one from Buckingham Palace.

'Do tell me who these lovely ladies are,' Darcia had begged her partner as the music stopped.

'There is no-one as lovely as you!' he had answered with a sincerity that was very flattering.

'Thank you,' Darcia replied, 'but as I am new to London I find it annoying not to be able to put a name to the faces I see night after night.'

Her partner had smiled but because he knew it was what she wanted he pointed out the most attractive women in the room one by one.

Because he had a slightly spiteful tongue he added something amusing, and at the same time usually unkind, about each one.

'Lovely – but nit-witted! Enchanting – but adores the sound of her own voice! Beautiful – but interested only in her own reflection!'

Darcia listened and egged him on until he said as she indicated a very beautiful blonde:

'That is Lady Caroline Blakeley, daughter of the Duke of Hull.'

'She is certainly very lovely,' Darcia remarked.

'She has hidden depths which are well beneath the surface.'

Darcia wondered exactly what he meant by that, but she did not ask the question. Instead she asked:

'Is she engaged to the good-looking man with whom she is dancing?'

'No, that is Lord Arkleigh. They say that Lady Caroline has an understanding, if that is the right word, with the Earl of Kirkhampton.'

'Then why has the engagement not been announced?' Darcia asked innocently.

'He is building a house for her. From all accounts it is taking him an unconscionable time to finish it.'

'That sounds rather dull,' Darcia said. 'If I were in love I would not want to wait for anything, even for a roof over my head.'

'If you fall in love with me,' her partner said, 'I promise you I will whisk you up the aisle before you can even draw in your breath!'

She had laughed at him but by the end of the evening she realised that his protestations of devotions were already beginning to bore her.

She was tired but could not sleep. All she could see in the darkness was the Earl as she had last seen him riding down the Row, the intent expression on his face as he flashed past.

Then there was another face, very clear, almost as if it was developed like one of the new photographs everyone was talking about, out of the darkness.

It was the face of Lady Caroline Blakeley with her fair skin and blue eyes the colour of forget-me-nots.

'She is very pretty,' Darcia told herself and knew that she was cheating because the right word was 'lovely'.

The following day it was impossible to do anything but what the *Marquise* expected her to do and the next day and the day after that were the same.

Then, two days before her own Ball the opportunity for which Darcia had been waiting came.

The *Marquise* sent her a message first thing in the morning to say she was indisposed.

Darcia went immediately to her room.

The blinds were drawn and there was the scent of Eau de Cologne on the air.

'I am so sorry, my dear,' the *Marquise*

apologised weakly, 'but I have one of my tiresome migraines. I have them occasionally, and there is nothing I can do but lie still until they go away.'

'I understand,' Darcia said sympathetically. 'You are certain there is nothing I can get you?'

'Nothing,' the *Marquise* replied painfully.

She obviously did not wish to talk and Darcia left the room.

Once back in her own bedroom she scribbled a note to Mr Curtis and started to dress hastily.

When she came downstairs she found as she had ordered there was a closed carriage waiting outside the front door and Mr Curtis had a sheet of paper in his hand which told her all she wished to know.

'You do not want me to come with you, *Mademoiselle?*' he asked.

Darcia shook her head and said in a voice which could be heard by the footmen:

'Thank you, Mr Curtis, I am going to visit an old lady I once knew who lives in the country. I am hoping she will be well enough to see me.'

'I hope so too, *Mademoiselle*,' Mr Curtis replied politely.

'Please cancel our engagements for today,'

Darcia went on, 'and ask the hostess with whom the *Marquise* and I were to dine tonight whether I can join her party alone...'

Without waiting for Mr Curtis's reply Darcia stepped into the carriage that was waiting outside and felt as it drove off, an excitement that she had not felt before any of the parties she had been to since she arrived in London.

As she was well aware it was not very far to Letty Green which because it lay on the very edge of her father's estate, was ten miles nearer to London than Rowley Park itself.

The Governess who had taught her for four years had been an elderly woman nine years ago when she had retired, and Darcia remembered her cottage was larger than the others in the village and stood in a neat, tidy little garden, which had always seemed to her to be rather like a doll's house.

When the horses drew up outside it an hour after they had left London, Darcia thought that her memory was very accurate, except that the garden was very much more overgrown than it had been when she had last seen it.

She stepped out, knocked on the white-painted front door, noting as she did so, that the knocker wanted cleaning.

It was some minutes before there was any answer and she was just going to knock again when the door opened and an elderly woman stood there who looked, Darcia thought, as if she came from the village.

'I would like to see Miss Graythorn,' she said, 'if it is convenient.'

'That's somethin' you can't do, Ma'am,' the woman answered in a broad country accent.

'Why not?' Darcia enquired.

''Cause her were buried last week,' the woman answered. 'I've just been a-wondering what to do about the house.'

Darcia walked further into the small hall and the woman shutting the door behind her opened the door into the Sitting-Room.

It was a very pleasant room, the windows looking onto the garden, and Darcia recognised immediately a number of things which Miss Graythorn had been allowed to take away with her from Rowley Park.

There hung on the walls neatly framed sketches Darcia had made in water colours when she was a child, and she found it rather touching that Miss Graythorn had treasured them.

'Tell me what happened,' she asked the woman from the village.

She then had to listen to a long, rambling story of how Miss Graythorn had been in failing health with no-one to look after her except the woman who was telling the tale.

'Has she no relatives?' Darcia asked when they finally reached Miss Graythorn's death and the Funeral.

'Not that I hears of,' the woman replied, 'an' no-one comes to visit her these last years.'

'Has she left any instructions?'

'That's just what I was a-wondering about,' the woman said. 'There's a letter here addressed to His Lordship's daughter, the Honourable Darcia Rowley. They tells I she's abroad somewhere, so I can't send it, can I?'

She spoke almost aggressively as if she was afraid of being accused of not doing her duty.

'No, that would be difficult,' Darcia agreed soothingly, 'but as Miss Darcia is a friend of mine, if you will give me the letter I promise she will receive it.'

She waited while the woman went to a French *secretaire* which stood against one of the walls, opened it and brought out a letter which was addressed in rather wavering hand-writing.

'Thank you,' Darcia said, 'and as I know Miss Darcia so well, I feel she would wish me to pay you for any work you have done since Miss Graythorn died, and to reimburse you for anything you have spent while she was ill.'

The woman's face wreathed in smiles.

'That's real kind of you, Ma'am,' she replied. 'I were wonderin' what I'd do about keeping the cottage clean. The trouble is I'll have to find another job. Money's useful when there's a large family.'

'Yes, I am sure it is,' Darcia answered.

She opened her bag and drew out three sovereigns.

'This should cover what you are owed and carry you over until I come again.'

The woman took the sovereigns incredulously as if she could hardly believe her good fortune.

'I might even wish to use a cottage until Miss Darcia returns to England,' Darcia said. 'In the meantime I will tell her how well you are looking after everything so that she will not worry.'

'There's no need to worry,' the woman said.

'What is your name?' Darcia enquired.

'Mrs Cosnett, Ma'am, and me husband's bin keeping the garden tidy. Comes twice a week, he does, as regular as regular.'

Darcia left some money for Mr Cosnett, then asked to be shown round the rest of the house.

She found each room was as well furnished as the small Sitting-Room, and thought it was typical of her father's openhanded generosity that he should not only have provided her old Governess with a roof over her head, but had also furnished her home in a style and extravagance that few women in such a position would expect in their wildest dreams.

The carpets being finely woven had stood the test of years, and the curtains still looked fresh and were for the most part unfaded.

The chairs, the chests, the tables and the grandfather-clock ticking in the hall were all fine enough to grace any house either in London or Paris.

'She certainly has some very fine things here,' Darcia said as they went downstairs again to the little hall, 'and it is lucky Miss Graythorn had you, Mrs Cosnett, to keep them so well and undamaged.'

'I often says to myself it's a responsibility,' Mrs Cosnett replied, then she gave a little cry.

'Oh! There's one thing I'd like to show you, Miss, and wish you'd mention it to Miss Darcia.'

'What is that?'

Mrs Cosnett led the way into the garden where there was a well built shed.

The roof was tiled and in good repair, and she saw that the door like the rest of the cottage, had been newly painted.

She did not know what she expected to find inside but when Mrs Cosnett opened the door she stared in astonishment.

'It were on its way three year ago to Rowley Park,' Mrs Cosnett explained, 'but there were an accident in the village, and Miss Graythorn 'as it brought in here for safety.

'"It won't hurt in there, Mrs Cosnett," she says to me, "and they'll be sending for it when they want it." But they never did, and here it still is!'

Darcia stared at the contents of what lay in front of her and knew exactly what it was.

It was the panelling which her father had bought from a house in Paris which had once belonged to the *Duc* de Richelieu.

It had been demolished and he had purchased the exquisitely carved panels and sent them to England.

'What will you do with it, Papa?' she had asked him.

'They were a bargain,' Lord Rowley explained, 'and they reminded me of the great Cardinal whose life has always fascinated me.'

'What will you do with French panelling in a house that is essentially English?' Darcia persisted.

Her father had shrugged his shoulders.

'It will come in useful some time,' he replied and Darcia had teased him for being unnecessarily extravagant.

Now she looked at the panelling and thought it was even more beautiful than she remembered it.

It struck her then that Fate had played into her hands in a strange and almost eerie fashion.

Here before her eyes was panelling that anyone who was building a house would be thrilled to have.

Panelling that was not only beautiful in itself but had great historical connections.

It was almost as if something stronger than herself was taking a hand in the game she had been playing quietly and secretly, and she knew she was not going to refuse such august assistance.

She looked and saw that most of the panels were long, made to stretch from the dado to just below the ceiling. Her eyes then lighted on a smaller one that was obviously meant for an over-door.

'I wonder, Mrs Cosnett,' she said aloud, 'if your husband would be kind enough to carry that panel out to the carriage? I can see he is working in the garden, and if it is too heavy there is a footman who can help him.'

'I be sure me husband'll manage, Ma'am,' Mrs Cosnett replied, and hurried off to call him.

CHAPTER THREE

The horses drawing the carriage in which Darcia was sitting began to move more slowly up the steep incline.

Half way up there was a gap in the trees which bordered the rough drive and she had her first sight of the house for which she was looking.

She had certainly because it was being built by the Earl, expected it to be impressive, but not in the least to resemble the building which she saw in front of her.

She had imagined, because he was tall and had the look of a Georgian Buck about him similar to the portraits that adorned the walls at Rowley Park, that his taste would be Georgian.

She had pictured a Palladian house with its wings attached to a lofty centre building, a porticoed front, and doubtless when it was finished statues and urns on the roof which would be silhouetted against the sky.

Instead she drew in her breath as she saw in front of her a house which seemed at first sight to be strangely familiar.

She thought it was exactly as she had imagined in her childhood dreams the Castle belonging to Prince Charming would look.

Then suddenly as the horses plodded on she knew why she felt as if she recognised it.

Because her father had such exquisite and at the same time cosmopolitan taste, he had made Darcia from an early age, appreciate the different style of buildings in every country they visited, the Piazzas in Venice, Palaces in Rome, and of course the Chateaux in France.

Lord Rowley had been particularly impressed by the ancient Chateaux of Valais and also by the great Chateaux of Touraine.

In front of her Darcia could recognise now their characteristic architecture, and she was sure as she drew nearer that the towers that surmounted the building ahead were replicas of those of Maintenon, the Chateau of the *Duc* de Noailles.

She was so surprised that such a building should be erected by an Englishman that she wondered if in fact, she had come to the wrong place.

Then as she saw that it was still unfinished, that there were piles of planks and stones, and workmen moving about, she knew that this was in fact the creation of the man in whom she was interested.

The carriage came to a standstill and the footman got down from the box to say as he opened the door:

'The coachman is afraid to go any further, *M'mselle,* as they have been digging in the road ahead.'

'Then wait here,' Darcia replied.

She stepped out and walked across the uneven ground, seeing as she expected that portions of it had been dug up to insert pipes or drains and it would in fact have been impossible for the carriage wheels to move safely.

She went to the front door and stood for a moment staring up at the house, impressed not only by its towers, but by its strangely shaped chimneys and the fine design of the roof.

She recognised what she thought were features that had been 'borrowed' from Blois and Chambord, and thought with a smile that the Earl was obviously determined to combine all the best features of French architecture in one building.

Intrigued and at the same time excited, she walked up several steps and in through the open front door.

She found herself in an oval Hall with an inlaid marble floor which looked as if it had just been completed.

She turned left moving along a Gallery with three windows overlooking the front of the house until she came to a small square room and saw that inside it was the man she sought.

He was standing sideways to her looking at a plan that was laid out on a plain deal table which stood in the centre of the room.

There was no mistaking the fineness of his features and the athletic grace of his body.

He must have sensed her presence for he did not raise his head but asked:

'What are your suggestions for this room? I see you have made none on the plan.'

The question was so apt that once again Darcia thought that Fate – or was it the luck her father had always attracted? – was hers too.

How could she imagine when she had left London that she would find the panels from the *Duc* de Richelieu's house in a shed in Letty Green, or that they could prove so completely appropriate to the house the Earl was building?

She did not however speak, and after a few

seconds the Earl raised his head as if to question her silence and saw her.

He looked at her in surprise, then said:

'I thought you were my decorator.'

Darcia moved slowly towards him.

She had taken great care before she left London not to wear one of the new extravagant and rather flamboyant gowns which she had bought in Paris.

Instead to her lady's-maid's disgust she had insisted on putting on one of the simple muslin dresses she had worn when she was at School.

It made her look very lovely, and perhaps because it was unornamented it accentuated the beauty of her hair and the largeness of her eyes.

'Please forgive me ... My Lord,' she said in a small hesitant voice as she reached the Earl's side, 'but I have brought ... something here with me which I think will ... interest you.'

The Earl raised his eye-brows before he replied:

'The only things which interest me at the moment are those that concern my house.'

'That is what I thought you would say,' Darcia replied, 'and what I would like to offer you would ... I feel, be absolutely ...

suitable for the room we are now in.'

She thought she saw a sceptical look in the Earl's eyes as if he had already been importuned by a great number of people wishing to sell him anything and everything on which they could make a profit.

'Of course,' Darcia said quickly, again in a self-deprecating manner which she was sure was the right way to approach him, 'you may ... already have the ... panelling you require?'

'Panelling?' the Earl enquired. 'Did you say panelling?'

'I have for sale, My Lord, panelling which was in the *Duc* de Richelieu's house in Paris before it was demolished.'

The Earl stared at her in astonishment before he said:

'Is that possible?'

Then a smile seemed to transform his face as he said:

'I think I must be dreaming and you are part of it. For over a week I have been worried about what I should do with this room, and now I know it must be panelling, and it must be French.'

'I have brought a small panel in my carriage, My Lord.'

The Earl walked to a door on the other

side of the room.

There must have been workmen in the next room because Darcia heard him say:

'Collect a panel of carving from the carriage you will find outside and bring it to me.'

There was the sound of footsteps clattering over the uncovered floor and the Earl returned.

'I feel I should ask you to sit down,' he said, 'but as you can see we are lamentably short of chairs at the moment.'

'May I look at your plans?' Darcia asked. 'And may I congratulate you on the most beautiful building I have ever seen outside France?'

'You have been to France?'

'Yes, and I have studied the Chateaux of Valais and the grand Chateaux of Touraine.'

'Then you will recognise quite a number of their features here.'

'I was sure I could not have been mistaken.'

'I found them so beautiful,' the Earl said, 'that I knew that if I was to build a house of my own I must incorporate everything that had moved and inspired me there.'

He gave a little laugh.

'Everybody told me I was making a

mistake, but now your congratulations tell me I was right.'

'Of course you were right!' Darcia said, 'and I think it very courageous and original of you to do what you want rather than be influenced by other people.'

The Earl seemed pleased by what she had said, but his eyes were on the plans that lay on the table.

There was one of the outside of the house which Darcia saw had been followed exactly, and there was also a plan of the inside on which were written suggested colours for the walls, besides some notes on furniture and fittings.

She found the room they were in and saw it was labelled 'The Breakfast Room', while the room through which she had reached it was 'The East Gallery'.

'I was trying to decide when you came,' the Earl said, 'what colour these rooms should be painted and what pictures would be most appropriate.'

He followed the plan of the room with his finger as he said:

'I was in fact thinking that this room was too small for pictures of any size, and yet I had no wish to leave the walls bare. Then you appeared!'

'I am sure,' Darcia said, 'that there will be just enough panelling to complete this room, and if you do not wish to have pictures here, with which I agree, then I think you need a very fine mirror over the mantelpiece.'

She paused before she added:

'It should reflect a large crystal chandelier which should hang from the ceiling in the centre of the room.'

The Earl stared at her.

'I do not believe what I am hearing!' he said. 'You seem to be not only part of a dream, but a magician who can read my thoughts.'

As he spoke there were footsteps in the East Gallery and a moment later two workmen carrying the panel from Darcia's carriage brought it into the room.

They set it down without being told against a wall which faced the window and in the light the Earl could see the exquisite golden bronze of the mellowed oak on which the delicate 17th century angels had been carved.

The men having done what they had been ordered to do disappeared, and Darcia waited while the Earl stood staring at the panel as if he expected it to vanish in front of his eyes.

Then he asked:

'You have a whole room of this?'

'Yes.'

'There is no point in my telling you that it is perfect! I can imagine nothing that would fit better into the house almost as if it had been made for it.'

As he spoke he gently touched the panel with his finger. Then he said:

'You must think me very rude, but I have not yet asked your name, or enquired why you came to me.'

Before Darcia could answer he added:

'It is obvious that in some magical way you sensed my need of you, but perhaps you also have a name.'

'It is Darcia.'

He raised his eye-brows.

'Is that all?'

'All that is important.'

He looked at her in a puzzled manner, then at the panelling.

'Is there perhaps something mysterious about the ownership of what you have brought me? Because even if it is stolen, smuggled or an illegal purchase, I still want it.'

Darcia laughed, and the sound seemed

like the song of birds as it echoed around the small room.

'It is none of those things, My Lord. It is just that I have called on you without a chaperon and without anyone being aware of my intentions.'

'I am most grateful,' the Earl said, 'and let me assure you, Miss Darcia, that I will keep your secret and will not betray you.'

'Thank you.'

'And the panelling is yours to sell?'

'There is no doubt about that.'

'Then it only remains for me to ask the price.'

Darcia made a little gesture with her hands.

'What is it worth to you?' she enquired.

'More than I can possibly afford!' the Earl replied, and they both laughed.

'As I have other ideas which might suit your very beautiful and imaginative house,' Darcia said, 'would it be inquisitive if I asked to see it?'

'Nothing would give me greater pleasure!' the Earl replied.

He picked up the plans from the table and carrying them under his arm led the way through the door on the other side of the room which she found led first into a

Conservatory, then into a large and very well proportioned Salon.

'This will be the Dining-Room,' the Earl said, 'and I shall be interested to know how you would decorate it.'

Darcia looked around.

There was already an exquisitely carved stone mantelpiece and three windows which looked onto the garden.

The Earl was waiting for her reply and she had the strange feeling he had been right when he had said she could read his thoughts.

It was almost as if she had tuned into his mind and she had not to think, but to listen.

'Well?' he asked after a moment.

'You have some tapestries?' she replied.

'Has someone been talking to you about my possessions?' he enquired sharply.

Darcia shook her head.

'To be honest I did not know you had any.'

'Then what do you know about me?'

'Only that your family mansion was burned down and you were building a house nearer to London.'

'Then let me inform you that one of the treasures saved from the Kirkhampton House was the Beauvais tapestries designed by Boucher.'

'No-one told me that,' Darcia said positively, 'but of course, that is why you designed this room this particular shape, and they will look magnificent here. And with them you will need an Aubusson carpet.'

'You are frightening me!' the Earl said briefly and he walked on.

The next room, which Darcia found lay behind the oval hall through which she had entered, was to be a Drawing-Room, and already it had a painted ceiling and a cornice of heavy gold leaf.

She looked around thinking how perfect the proportions were and the Earl said:

'I hardly dare to ask you on this, but what colour would you choose for the walls?'

'You may be shocked or surprised at my reply,' Darcia answered, 'but I think red silk brocade would make a perfect background for the pictures which this room needs.'

The Earl walked to the window to stand looking out.

'Come here!' he said.

She walked to his side and he pointed at the view which, as she anticipated, was fantastic.

Immediately below the hill on which the house stood the ground sloped gradually away into a flat plain that stretched to a hazy horizon.

Bathed in the spring sunshine it looked so beautiful that Darcia could only stand looking at it and feeling there were no words with which to describe anything so lovely.

'I was a small boy when I first saw this view,' the Earl said at her side. 'I was out hunting with my father. We came here following a fox which had eluded the hounds all day. We stood about for a little while in the woods, and as I was beginning to feel cold, I trotted off on my own just with a desire to keep moving. Then suddenly I saw this view below me and as I looked the sun came out illuminating the scene.'

There was silence before the Earl said:

'It was almost as if a voice told me that one day I would come back, one day this view would belong to me.'

'I think,' Darcia replied after a moment, 'that whether or not you built this house or whether you lived elsewhere the view would still have been … yours.'

She knew he did not understand and went on:

'Whenever we see anything beautiful such as this is, or hear music that raises our minds and our senses, it becomes part of ourselves and is something we can never lose.'

'Who told you that?' the Earl asked sharply.

Darcia gave him a little smile.

'I imagine I thought it out for myself,' she replied, 'but I am also sure that sooner or later everybody who thinks comes to the same conclusion.'

The Earl was about to say something, then he changed his mind. Instead he drew his watch from his waist-coat pocket and said:

'As time is getting on, Miss Darcia, I think we should discuss our business, and if that is satisfactory, make arrangements to collect the panelling from wherever you may have it stored.'

The change in his voice was so sharp and so unexpected that for a moment Darcia felt almost as if he insulted her, then she understood.

She had frightened him, and he was feeling that because they thought alike there was something uncanny about it, something not natural.

She therefore answered him in exactly the same business-like way he had spoken to her.

'I quite understand, My Lord,' she said, 'and I must not take up too much of your valuable time. The rest of the panelling is in a village about two miles from here called Letty Green, and if you will arrange to have it collected some time tomorrow, I will see there is someone there to show your men where it is stored.'

'And the price?' the Earl enquired.

Darcia had brought too many things with her father on their travels not to have a very shrewd appreciation of what the panelling was worth.

She however named a sum that was reasonable without being so low that the Earl might have become suspicious as to her right of ownership.

He did not speak and she added:

'I dare say I could get more if I hawked it round London, but I need the money and do not wish to wait. The panelling being so near, My Lord, makes everything more convenient for both of us.'

'I can only accept your offer with pleasure,' the Earl replied. 'Would you like a cheque now, Miss Darcia, or should my men bring it with them tomorrow when they collect the rest of the panelling?'

'Tomorrow would be perfectly satisfactory,'

Darcia answered, 'and thank you for allowing me to contribute to this very beautiful building.'

She curtsied and put out her hand as if she would leave him, but the Earl said hastily:

'You said you might have other things. Have you anything particular in mind?'

'I have as it happens a number of pictures and some furniture as well,' Darcia replied, 'but I would of course, like to see more of the house before making suggestions.'

She knew as she spoke that she was punishing him for his impulse to be rid of her in case she encroached further on his thoughts and feelings that were too intimate to be shared by a stranger.

Before he could think about how to extricate himself from his own impetuosity she said:

'Perhaps you would permit me to call on another occasion? I have appointments over the next few days which will take up a great deal of my time.'

She noted the expression of concern which came into the Earl's eyes.

'If you mean you are selling treasures such as you have just sold me,' he said quickly, 'I should be grateful if I could have first refusal.'

'I am afraid I cannot make such a sweeping promise, My Lord,' Darcia said stiffly. 'After all, I only came here on an impulse, and, shall I confess, curiosity, to see what sort of house you were erecting.'

'And yet you brought a piece of the panelling with you!'

Darcia thought she might have suspected he would be astute enough to remember that.

'I was taking it to London which is where I am going now,' she replied.

The Earl gave an exclamation that was curiously like a groan.

'I cannot bear to think you might not have been curious,' he said, 'and came instead on another day when you had already sold the panelling.'

'I always think fate has a hand in everything we do and in everything that happens to us,' Darcia replied. 'So perhaps, My Lord, it was fate which made me decide to sell that particular panelling and to carry it with me when I was en route for London.'

'Even if fate is on my side today,' the Earl said, 'you must not let her fail me tomorrow. Please come again, Miss Darcia, and bring me anything that you think will fit into my house.'

'I will certainly think about it,' Darcia replied. 'Good-bye, My Lord.'

She curtsied again and moving quicker than he had expected she passed from the Drawing-Room into the Hall and before the Earl could catch up with her she had descended the steps and was outside in the sunshine.

As she reached the carriage she turned round to see him standing at the front door watching her.

She gave him a little wave of her hand, then without waiting for his response stepped into the carriage.

She longed to look back being sure he was watching her go, but instead she sat staring straight ahead of her, knowing that something strange and tremendous had happened in her life, and yet was afraid to assess accurately how important it would prove to be.

She drove first to Letty Green, found Mrs Cosnett still at the cottage, and told her the men would be coming the next day to collect the panelling from the shed in the garden.

'I'm glad ye've found a home for it, Ma'am,' Mrs Cosnett said, 'and to tell th' truth me husband has his eye on that shed for his tools.'

'I can see it will make a convenient place to keep them,' Darcia replied, 'and there's one thing I want to ask you, Mrs Cosnett.'

'What's that, Ma'am?'

'Will you make quite sure you do not mention Miss Darcia to the men who are coming?'

Mrs Cosnett looked surprised and Darcia explained:

'She has her reasons for not coming back to England for the moment, and she might not wish people to know that she was disposing of anything she owned.'

Darcia hoped Mrs Cosnett would not be too curious but she was surprised when a look of understanding came into her honest eyes.

'I understands, Ma'am, what you're saying,' she said, 'we all knows that His Lordship's living out o' England because of th' scandal that's being talked about him. Very nasty things has been said but Miss Graythorn always said as she didn't believe a half o' them!'

'I am sure Miss Graythorn was right,' Darcia replied. 'People exaggerate, Mrs Cosnett, and you know as well as I do that gossip can often be both unkind and untrue.'

Mrs Cosnett sighed and Darcia went on:

'Because Miss Darcia is a friend of mine I am hoping that the scandal about His Lordship will be forgotten so that they will be able to come back to England.'

'I can understand your feelings, Ma'am,' Mrs Cosnett said, 'an' there's a lot o' people around here as misses His Lordship. At the same time, they likes t' talk about him, brings a bit of colour, so t' speak into their lives.'

Darcia found it hard not to laugh.

That was true, she thought. Her father's escapades had brought colour and excitement and a sense of adventure to many people, and yet inevitably it had meant that he was exiled from his own home and so was she.

She left Mrs Cosnett, pleased with the thought that neither she nor her husband had to look for other work and promised to be back again within a week.

Then as she drove home she was making plans – plans which most certainly would have surprised the *Marquise* and would have positively alarmed the Earl!

In the next week there was not just one party every day but several, and Mr Curtis's list of her engagements seemed to grow and grow until Darcia almost groaned when she saw it.

'I have not time for any more parties,' she said, 'and less time to write letters. I am weeks behind with the people I have to thank for flowers and my dinner hostesses must take priority.'

'I wish that was something I could do for you, *Mademoiselle*,' Mr Curtis said.

'So do I!' Darcia replied in a heart-felt tone.

'You are not grumbling, *ma chère?*' the *Marquise* asked.

'Not really,' Darcia replied, 'but I want a day off to go and look at Rowley Park.'

'Is that wise? It will only upset you.'

'Not really, but it is important that no-one there should know who I am.'

She looked at Mr Curtis as she spoke, and he said:

'I anticipated you might raise that point, *Mademoiselle*. The caretakers are new, while the rest of the staff, as you may remember, were pensioned off and unless you call at their cottages they are not likely to see you.'

'That is what I wanted to know,' Darcia said. 'I will take the same carriage I had the other day and I would like it here at eleven o'clock tomorrow morning.'

'Darcia, Darcia, you are going too fast!' the *Marquise* exclaimed. 'We have promised to lunch with the Duchess of Bedford tomorrow.'

Darcia gave her a little smile as she answered:

'This is where your training in diplomacy comes in, but do not forget to tell me what excuse you have made before we dine with the French Ambassador.'

As she ran down the stairs punctually at the stroke of eleven the next morning she went off almost like a child going on her holidays.

It was a warm day and once again she was wearing a simple gown that was one of her school dresses, and her hat which was flat-brimmed to keep away the sun was trimmed only with a wreath of field flowers and some green ribbons which matched the colour of her eyes.

She looked very young and very lovely, and although she was unaware of it the footmen seeing her off in the carriage looked at her in admiration as she drove away.

She went first to Rowley Park and at the sight of the great house now empty and closed, she felt the tears come into her eyes.

She had always been so happy there as a child and she longed, as so many people have before her, to put back the clock.

She wished she were looking out of the Nursery window into the sunshine, knowing that as soon as she had finished breakfast she would go riding with her father.

There had also been long days when he had not been there, but causing raised eye-brows by his behaviour in London, or seeking diverse amusements on the Continent.

But he had always returned to her cries of delight, and then the house had seemed to come alive just because he was home.

The tempo would rise and everything would be so thrilling and exciting that time flew by on wings and there never seemed to be enough hours, minutes, seconds in the day.

The caretakers let her in and she walked through rooms where the furniture was covered with holland dust-sheets, the pictures shrouded, and there was no fragrance of flowers, but only the smell of dust and airlessness.

Darcia went from room to room knowing what she was seeking, and when finally she found it the caretaker lifted it down for her and placed it in her carriage.

Then she drove away knowing that the excitement she had been feeling in her breast ever since she left London had intensified and her heart seemed to be beating quicker and quicker.

It was almost intolerable how slowly the horses climbed the hill until there in front of her, even more beautiful than it had seemed the first time she saw it, was the Earl's house.

Now she did not see the piles of planks and stones, or the workmen, instead she had a vision of what it would be like when it was finished.

The green lawns sloping away would be like velvet, the shrubs in front of the windows covered in blossom and flower-beds laid out in traditional French style.

She felt as if she must dance as she moved towards the front door.

Then as she reached it and before she could climb the steps the Earl was there holding out his hand.

'You are here!' he cried. 'I was beginning to think I would never see you again! How could you stay away so long? How could you have forgotten that I wanted you?'

He took her hand in his and drew her

along the East Gallery with a speed that made her almost run beside him.

'It is finished! I had everybody working from the moment it arrived, and now I have only been waiting for you to see it.'

He took her into the Breakfast Room and when she saw the panelling on the walls she realised that he could not have found anything more perfect for the room in which it had been erected.

The cupids and the gold strapwork seemed to gleam in the light from the windows and she saw too that the chandelier she had suggested hung from the centre of the ceiling and looked exactly as she had thought it would.

The Earl was standing watching the expression on her face.

'It fits! It all fits in!'

Darcia clapped her hands.

'Perfectly, just as if it was made for it!' the Earl agreed. 'How can you have known – how can you have guessed that this was what I needed?'

She did not answer but looked up at the chandelier and he went on:

'Because I wanted the room to be complete when you came back I had it hung there at the same time and also the mirror where you suggested.'

Because she had stopped a few feet inside the door Darcia had not seen the mirror over the mantelpiece that was on her right.

Now she saw it was framed in gold as she had envisaged, and carved with cupids which echoed those depicted on the panels.

'It is as you hoped?' the Earl asked almost as if he was begging her to praise him.

'It is exactly as I saw this room in my imagination,' Darcia said quietly.

He gave a sigh as if of relief. Then he asked:

'Where do we go next? I realised after you left me that I should have insisted on your staying longer and demanded your help.'

Darcia gave a little laugh.

'I had the feeling that you resented it.'

'Why should you say that?' the Earl asked quickly.

Then as if he was compelled to be honest, he added:

'You are right, as usual. Yes, I felt almost as if you were taking over, and that if I was not careful I should not have a say in what until now has been exclusively mine.'

'I would not wish you to feel like that.'

'I know, I know,' he said, 'and afterwards I was furious with myself for being so stupid.'

'It is not exactly stupid to be possessive.'

'No, it can be egotistical, selfish, or merely a "dog-in-a-manger" attitude, but where you were concerned it was something I had never encountered before.'

'What do you mean by that?'

'I felt – how can I explain it? – as if you had supernatural powers in knowing what this house required, or magical, if you prefer.'

Darcia laughed.

'I am not a witch, if that is what you are implying.'

'Perhaps the idea was in the back of my mind,' the Earl answered.

'And now you have forgotten such fears?'

'I have convinced myself, Miss Darcia, that you are a very shrewd and clever business-woman. You know as well as I do that I am finding it impossible not to ask you, not to beg you, to tell me what else you have to sell and if it is what the house needs.'

'I am sure of it, but you make things rather difficult for me,' Darcia replied.

'In what way?'

'By refusing to show me more than two of your rooms.'

'Forgive me,' the Earl said, 'and do not

hold what I admit was inexcusable behaviour against me in the future.'

He thought that Darcia had not accepted his apology whole-heartedly and added:

'I will plead for your forgiveness in any way that you wish, on my knees, if necessary, but do not disappear again. Incidentally, I called at your cottage. The woman in charge of it told me that she had no idea when she would see you again. Can you imagine how anxious that made me?'

'Why should I have thought you would be anxious to see me?' Darcia asked wide-eyed. 'You were obviously in a hurry for me to leave the last time I was here.'

'Now you are being cruel and unkind,' the Earl said. 'I have already apologised for driving you away, and I have been severely punished. Can we not start again from the moment when fate brought you into my life?'

It was impossible, Darcia thought, to resist a man who looked so handsome and so attractive when he spoke to her with a sincerity which was inescapable.

'Because you are forgiven,' she replied, 'I will show you something you might like to see in my carriage.'

She saw the light in the Earl's eyes and

heard the excited note in his voice as he shouted for two workmen to bring him what was in the carriage inside the house.

When he left her she walked through the open door into the Conservatory and then into the Dining-Room.

Quite a lot of work had been done on the room since she was last there and she thought all it needed now was for the tapestries to be put in place and a chandelier hung from the ceiling.

There was however something still missing, and when the men brought what she had taken off the wall at Rowley Park into the room, the Earl gave a cry of delight.

It was a picture of three cupids painted by Boucher and Darcia knew that the colours, the exquisite flesh tints, and the charm of the cupids would complete a room that was to be hung with tapestries designed by the same master.

The Earl was gazing at the picture enraptured.

'I have searched everywhere for a picture like this,' he said. 'How can you have found it and to whom does it belong?'

'It belongs to me.'

'Now it may do,' he replied, 'but from whom did you acquire it?'

He waited for an answer and after a pause she said:

'I never reveal the names of my clients.'

'You are in business?'

She did not reply and he asked wonderingly:

'How can you do business alone when you are so young? Are you acting on behalf of your father or an employer?'

Darcia moved away from him towards the window to stand looking at the view and the Earl came to join her there.

'I want you to answer me,' he said.

'I think, My Lord,' she replied, 'that we both have secrets which we see no reason to share with strangers – or perhaps acquaintances is a better expression.'

'That is an absurd statement!'

'Why?'

She looked at him and knew that he was finding it impossible to put what he was feeling into words.

After a moment he said:

'I want us to be friends, Miss Darcia, and as a friend I need your help, your advice, and your amazing ability to bring me exactly what I need for my house.'

'That of course is business,' Darcia said quickly.

The Earl shook his head.

'Is it business that makes you know what I am thinking or what I am aiming at?' he enquired. 'Can you do the same with everyone to whom you are selling something? It would be extremely advantageous, but somehow I feel it is not true.'

'Why should you feel that?'

'I do not know,' he said. 'If you are able to be intuitive about me, then I can feel the same about you, and apart from your qualities which I think are magical I am also certain, although I have no real grounds for thinking so, that you are not what you seem!'

CHAPTER FOUR

They finished their tour of the First Floor having already seen on the Ground Floor another large Drawing-Room, the West Gallery, the Library and a room that the Earl said was to be exclusively his.

There were other rooms, but he said they were not ready for Darcia's inspection and instead took her upstairs where she found he had planned not only many delightful bedrooms, but also several bathrooms that she had not expected.

When they reached the Ground Floor again the Earl looked at her and said:

'I have the uneasy feeling that I have done something wrong.'

'Not exactly ... wrong,' Darcia said hesitatingly.

'I am preparing myself for a shock,' he said with a somewhat wry smile on his lips.

'You have planned your house with a perfection I find overwhelming,' she said, 'but it is the house of a bachelor.'

The Earl frowned, then he asked sharply:

'What do you mean by that?'

'You have forgotten that women, all women, need room for their clothes.'

The Earl put his hand up to his forehead.

'Do you mean cupboards?'

'I mean,' Darcia said, 'that too many wardrobes, which I have never thought are attractive pieces of furniture, would spoil the symmetry of your bedrooms, and it would be much more convenient for any ladies you entertain here to have wardrobe-room separate from their bedroom.'

The Earl gave an exclamation that was almost like a groan.

'You are right,' he said after a moment, 'and I think I hate you!'

Darcia laughed.

'You are not compelled to listen to my opinions.'

'There is nothing else I can do, and I realise you have found a flaw in my design which should have been obvious to me.'

'Let me look at the plans,' Darcia suggested.

As the Earl had left them in the Breakfast Room they walked back there and as they entered Darcia thought again how lovely the *Duc* de Richelieu's panelling looked and how perfectly it fitted into the room.

But she could not help wondering who would breakfast there with the Earl and what they would say to each other.

It was depressing to remember that he might be with his wife – the Beauty for whom he was building this house.

What she was thinking must have shown in her expression for the Earl said after a moment:

'You cannot be finding anything wrong with this room?'

'No, of course not!' Darcia said quickly. 'I was in fact, thinking of something quite different.'

'Think of me!' the Earl said insistently. 'Think of how much I need you to help me at this particular moment.'

Darcia felt almost as if she vibrated to what he was saying, then because she had no answer ready she turned to the plans finding beneath the sheet which showed the Ground Floor another for the bedrooms.

She saw the largest room was labelled 'The Master Bedroom' and knew that this was where the Earl would sleep either alone – or with his wife.

There was already a bathroom attached to it and on one side a dressing-room and on the other a *Boudoir*.

But no provision had been made for any cupboards and she knew that a huge, clumsy, unwieldy wardrobe, however decorative would spoil the room and look out of place among what she was certain would otherwise be French furniture.

Picking up a pencil she pointed to another room beyond the *Boudoir*.

'What are you planning for this room?' she asked.

'It is where I intend my most distinguished guest shall sleep,' the Earl replied.

'How unfortunate, for he or she will have to share it with gowns, bonnets, sun-shades and shoes!' Darcia said mockingly.

She drew a line down the middle of the room.

'There is the wardrobe-room for the Master Suite,' she said, 'and what is left is only large enough for a bachelor.'

'I will not have my plans...' the Earl began angrily, then unexpectedly he laughed.

'All right,' he exclaimed, 'you win! But if you create wardrobe-rooms all over the First Floor I shall have to build another wing.'

'Or reduce the size of your house-party!'

'The architect who did the working plan

from my own rough designs,' the Earl said, 'told me in no uncertain terms that one always built too small. He has prophesied truly, and I have the uneasy feeling that if I take your advice I shall not be building one wing, but several others as well!'

'There will also be the question of where your children will sleep when you have them,' Darcia said. 'You cannot "spoil the ship for a half-pennyworth of tar!"'

They both laughed, but as they did so, there was the sound of a high, feminine voice saying:

'Kindly tell me where I can find the Earl of Kirkhampton!'

Darcia started, then said to the Earl:

'I do not ... wish to be ... seen here.'

'No, of course not,' he answered.

He made a gesture with his hand towards the Conservatory, and as she moved quickly into it the Earl shut the door behind her, but she saw apprehensively that it had no lock, and it swung open.

Darcia put her hand against it to hold it in place, and as she did so, she heard a woman exclaim:

'Granby! Are you surprised to see me?'

'Very surprised, Caroline,' the Earl answered. 'Why did you not let me know you were coming?'

'I came to see what you were doing. Do you know it is over a month since you have been to London?'

'I have been busy,' the Earl replied, 'and when you see what has been achieved since you were last here you will understand why.'

'I am not interested in your silly old house, but in you.'

Darcia was well aware who had arrived. It was the beautiful Lady Caroline Blakeley whom she had seen at the Ball and thought that her golden hair, blue eyes and pink-and-white skin had a fairy-like quality which was undoubtedly suited to the house which the Earl was building for her.

'I am flattered!' the Earl said. 'At the same time I want you to love your future home as I love it already.'

'It is still in rather a mess,' Lady Caroline complained, 'I had to leave the carriage a little way down the drive. And, Granby, there is another carriage there. Who is visiting you?'

There was a sudden jealousy in her voice and Darcia held her breath as the Earl replied casually:

'I expect it belongs to the Architect or the decorator. They are both here somewhere in the building.'

As if he was anxious to keep off the subject he went on:

'Tell me what you think of this room. This is where we will start the day with breakfast, and which appropriately is the first room to be finished except for the carpet and curtains.'

'And I suppose the furniture,' Lady Caroline added.

'You like it?' the Earl asked eagerly.

'It is charming,' she said without any enthusiasm in her voice, 'but actually, Granby dear, I shall have breakfast in my own room, as I always do.'

'Even in the country?'

'Even in the country.'

'Then let me show you some of the other rooms,' the Earl suggested.

Darcia was sure that he was disappointed by Lady Caroline's lack of enthusiasm about the room with which he himself was so pleased.

'I have very little time,' Lady Caroline replied. 'I came especially to ask you, Granby, if you will accompany me to the Masked Ball which the Russian Ambassador is giving at the end of the week.'

Now there was a note of excitement in her

voice as she said:

'I thought it would be amusing if we went dressed as two famous Russian characters, perhaps Queen Catherine and Count Orlov?'

The Earl did not reply and she continued:

'If we arrived in a sleigh – we would have one built on wheels – and a servant dressed in period costume pushed us into the Ball-Room, it would be sensational!'

There was silence while she obviously waited for an answer. Then the Earl said:

'I am sorry to disappoint you, Caroline, but if there is one thing I dislike it is dressing up to make a fool of myself. Besides I really have not the time at the moment for Balls.'

'I am asking you, Granby, to come with me.'

There was a note of steel in Lady Caroline's voice.

'We will dine together next week or the week after,' the Earl replied, 'but certainly not the night of the Ball.'

Lady Caroline stamped her foot.

'Really, Granby! You are being extremely irritating and, I may point out, neglectful.'

'I have no wish to be that,' the Earl answered. 'After all, I am building this house for you.'

'The house! Always the house!' Lady Caroline cried. 'Can you not understand that I want you – not a lot of bricks and mortar? There are plenty of houses you could have bought for half the money you are spending on this.'

'Do you really imagine I want somebody else's house built to suit someone else's taste?' the Earl enquired.

'What does it matter what a house looks like outside?' Lady Caroline enquired. 'As long as it is comfortable, luxurious, and can accommodate our friends, its actual appearance does not matter.'

The Earl did not speak, but Darcia could imagine that he was pressing his lips together in a tight line.

'While you are fussing over this house,' Lady Caroline went on, 'you are neglecting me, and people are talking.'

'So that is what is disturbing you!'

'Of course it is! It did not matter during the winter, when you were away so much, but now in the Season when I need an escort at the Balls, the Opera, and Receptions by the dozen, it is extremely galling to have people continually asking me where you are and what you are doing.'

116

'They should know where by this time.'

'When I tell them the truth they do not believe me!' Lady Caroline snapped. 'I am quite certain the majority of our friends think you have some fair charmer hidden away here in the woods whom you find more enticing than me!'

Lady Caroline looked up at the Earl with her blue eyes as she spoke, and was so lovely that he exclaimed:

'You know that is impossible!'

'That is what I wished you to say, Granby! So prove that you still love me by coming back with me to London.'

The Earl did not reply and she moved a little closer to him.

'Your house is waiting for you, and if it pleases you we could dine there tonight. Mama would be horrified if she knew about it, but I will pretend you have a large party, and that I shall be well chaperoned.'

Lady Caroline moved even closer to the Earl and now as if he could not resist the perfection of her lips or the enticement in her eyes, he put his arms around her.

'You are not to kiss me,' she whispered, 'unless you promise to give me dinner this evening.'

The Earl did not answer, he merely took

possession of her mouth and there was silence for what seemed to Darcia to be a long time.

He raised his head and said:

'We will dine together and if you go back to London now, I will follow in an hour or so with my own horses.'

'You are very sweet to me, Granby dear,' Lady Caroline said, 'and there is so much I want to talk to you about tonight.'

Her voice was very beguiling as she added hardly above a whisper: 'and especially about our wedding.'

'That will be as soon as the house is finished.'

'And when will that be?'

'In perhaps five or six months.'

'It is too long to wait. I wish for a summer wedding.'

There was silence. Then the Earl said:

'We cannot talk about it now.'

'I feel sure, Granby – dear Granby – you will give me what I want.'

The Earl did not answer and Lady Caroline said hastily:

'Come with me to my carriage and see me off.'

Because she could not resist having one quick glance at the woman she had only seen once before Darcia allowed the door into the Breakfast Room to open just a fraction.

The Earl had his back to her, but Lady Caroline was at that moment slipping her arm through his, her lovely face with its almost classical features lifted towards him, her eyes very blue in the sunshine from the windows.

She was beautifully dressed and was, Darcia thought, exactly like a Dresden china figure. She would undoubtedly fit perfectly into the Dining-Room with its Boucher picture and tapestries.

She watched the Earl and Lady Caroline walk from the Breakfast Room and heard their voices receding gradually into the distance as they moved along the East Gallery.

Then she left the door of the Conservatory open and moved into the Dining-Room to stare up at the picture of the Boucher angels which the Earl had already hung over the mantelpiece.

'Why should I let that go to her when it means nothing?' Darcia asked herself bitterly.

Even while she knew the answer she could not for the moment prevent the agony of what she overheard from stabbing her like a thousand knives.

Then she told herself that somehow she would save the Earl from a woman who was not interested in the house he had built for her or, Darcia thought perceptively, in the Earl as the man he really was.

Just as she had found herself knowing intuitively what he wanted, and even what he thought, she was sure now that Lady Caroline's protestations of affection were insincere.

There was something behind her insistence that he must be with her in London.

She suddenly remembered how the first night when Lady Caroline had been pointed out to her the man who had done so had said she had 'hidden depths beneath the surface.'

What were they? Darcia wondered, and how could she find out the secrets that she was obviously hiding from the man who loved her?

At the same time it was not surprising.

There was no doubt that Lady Caroline was beautiful, a conventional, very English beauty, but still the type that artists had portrayed since the beginning of time, and men of every nationality found irresistible.

'She is lovely, very lovely!' Darcia admitted despondently.

As she said the words beneath her breath she heard the Earl coming through the Conservatory towards her.

She turned to look at him and as the sunshine glittered on the glass behind him it made him appear as if he was haloed with a light and gave him the appearance of a Divinity rather than a man.

It was then Darcia knew in the flash of a second that she would fight for him and that no-one, even the most beautiful woman in the world, would take him from her.

It was as if all her thoughts and feelings for him over the years were suddenly crystallised into the knowledge that she not only loved him but already belonged to him.

He was hers, and she had recognised him all those years ago when she had first seen him sitting at her father's dining-table, and when he had opened the door for her as she left to go to bed.

'I love him!' her heart throbbed.

She knew it was not the ordinary love of a woman for a handsome man, but something different and more fundamental, the recognition of the other half of herself, across an eternity of time.

'I must apologise for the interruption,' the Earl said politely as he joined her.

'I am perhaps taking up too much of your time,' Darcia suggested humbly.

'No, that is not true,' the Earl replied, 'and now that I have waited for you for so long, there are thousands of questions as yet unanswered, so you cannot speak of leaving.'

Darcia hesitated a moment. Then she said:

'Actually I am in no hurry, but as I cannot get to London early I was wondering if you would think it very rude if I had something to eat before we did anything else.'

The Earl gave an exclamation.

'How can I be so inhospitable as not to think you might be hungry?' he exclaimed. 'But I am afraid I eat very little or nothing when I am engrossed with the house. And perhaps one of my servants…'

Darcia put up her hand to stop what he was about to suggest.

'I have with me a picnic luncheon,' she said, 'and I should be very honoured if you would join me.'

'You are the most efficient woman I have ever met,' the Earl replied, 'and I am delighted to accept your invitation.'

Darcia gave him a smile.

'The food is in my carriage and as it is such a lovely day could we eat in the garden?'

'There is nothing I would like better,' the Earl answered.

They walked together towards the carriage and Darcia told the footman to carry the large picnic-basket she had brought with her to where the Earl directed.

He led the way through some rhododendrons ablaze with crimson blossoms. There was a clear piece of ground surrounded by trees and shrubs and at one point there was a view over the valley that was also to be seen from the house.

'This is superb!' Darcia exclaimed. 'First we can sit in the shade of the trees.'

The footman laid two carriage-rugs down on the grass, and Darcia began to unpack the hamper while the Earl sat on one of the rugs and watched her.

'Your visitor stayed a very short time,' Darcia remarked as she took out the covered silver dishes which the French Chef the *Marquise* employed in London had filled with exotic and delicious food.

'The lady in question was in a hurry,' the Earl replied.

There was a pause, then he asked:

'Why did you insist on hiding yourself?'

'I have reasons for not wishing people to know what is essentially my business.'

'That tells me nothing,' the Earl answered. 'Why should you be so mysterious? Do you realise I do not even know your name?'

'I told you – I answer to Darcia.'

'Supposing I had to write to you?'

'You know where my cottage is.'

'It does not look like your cottage,' the Earl remarked, 'I saw there were some lovely things in it, but it is not the type of background in which I envisage you.'

'I cannot imagine why you should concern yourself with my background.'

'If you set out to intrigue me, to make me determined to find out who you are, why you came to me, and what is your real name, you could not have been more clever about it!'

'If you are trying to catch me out and force some sort of confession from my lips,' Darcia said, 'please let us eat first, then perhaps I shall be quicker-witted than I feel at the moment.'

'I have never known you to be anything else!' the Earl flashed.

She laughed and passed him a pâté which

he looked at, then remarked:

'I suppose I should not be surprised that with your amazing sense of what is right, you have now produced a superlative meal.'

'I only hope the wine is right too,' Darcia answered. 'Women are supposed to be lamentably ignorant at choosing what a man prefers to drink.'

The Earl looked to where a bottle of wine stood in a silver ice-cooler which the footman had brought and set down beside them while they were talking.

He poured a little wine into a glass, sipped it and said:

'Perfect! And may I say despite your pretended modesty, Darcia, I was quite certain that you knew it would be.'

Darcia noticed the way he addressed her but made no comment, and the Earl filled both their glasses. Then rising he said:

'To someone who attempts to be like the Sphinx and instead looks as if she has stepped down from Olympus.'

He drank a little of the wine from his glass and said:

'Sheer nectar! Is that what you are?'

'A goddess from Olympus?' Darcia queried. 'I wish it were true, but the only goddesses who you need should be on the walls of your house.'

'I feel you have a reason for that remark. What are you suggesting?'

Darcia smiled.

'I was thinking that you needed a goddess for the large Drawing-Room.'

There was a look of excitement in the Earl's eyes as he enquired:

'Which one?'

'I was thinking for the larger wall a picture called *"Venus, Mercury and Cupid"*, by Louis Michel Van Loo!'

For a moment he stared at her incredulously, as if he could not believe what she had said. Then he asked quickly:

'Are you telling me that it would be possible for you to obtain that picture for me?'

'If you would like it.'

'If I would like it!' the Earl repeated. 'It is a picture I have longed to see, but had no idea where it was or to whom it belonged.'

'It has just the colouring which I think you need for that room,' Darcia said. 'The flesh tints of Venus come across so admirably with the darker, warm hues of Mercury, and the Cupid at his knee is very attractive.'

'I have seen a reproduction of it somewhere,' the Earl said, 'but not a good one.'

'Then I am sure it would give that Drawing-Room a focal point around which all the other decorations could be chosen.'

The Earl sat up and she knew he was seeing exactly what she was conveying to him.

'When can I have this picture?'

'You are sure you want it?'

'Are you really asking me such a foolish question? You know I want it as swiftly as you can bring it to me, or would you prefer me to collect it?'

'Are you being helpful – or inquisitive?' Darcia questioned.

The Earl laughed.

'It did strike me that it would be a way of getting to know where you keep this store-house of treasures. I am well aware that the *Venus, Mercury and Cupid* will be too big for that little cottage you tell me is yours in Letty Green.'

'I will bring it to you tomorrow,' Darcia promised, 'unless you would rather wait until later on in the week?'

There was just a pause and she knew that the Earl was thinking that Lady Caroline would expect him to stay in London tomorrow after they had dined together tonight.

He made up his mind.

'I will be back here at noon.'

'Then I will arrange for the picture to be with you at that time,' Darcia said.

'And you will come with it?'

'I am not sure,' she answered. 'It might be difficult for me.'

'What do you mean – difficult?' the Earl enquired. 'Who else has demands on your time?'

'You have no right to ask such a question.'

'But because you have an interest in my house you will give me an answer,' the Earl said. 'And now you have come back to me, let me make it quite clear that I will not be content with one picture, I want a great deal more.'

'How much more?'

'I am waiting for you to tell me that.'

'You are aware I must be very careful so as not to let you think I am taking the house away from you?' she teased.

'I was crazy the first day we met,' the Earl admitted, 'but it is difficult to explain why I was suddenly afraid of you, and your intuition, or whatever you like to call it.'

Darcia did not reply, she merely helped herself from another dish that was even more delicious than the last.

'Now,' the Earl went on as if he was feeling

for words, 'you express exactly what is in my mind and dreams. Could anything be a better partnership?'

Darcia felt her heart leap at his words, but she was careful to give no indication of it. Instead she said:

'I have no wish to impose myself upon you, My Lord, but...'

The Earl waited. Then he said:

'I would like you to finish that sentence.'

'...but I find your house,' Darcia said softly, 'so exciting, so enchanting and at the same time so inspiring, that I want to help you bring it to the perfection it deserves.'

'That is what it will have,' the Earl said positively. 'But let me make this clear once and for all: I need you! In fact I am beginning to think that I cannot do without you.'

She looked at him trying to make her expression one of impersonal enquiry, but somehow she found her eyes were held by his and it was difficult to look away.

Then with an effort she said:

'You are eating nothing, and Chef will be so disappointed.'

She had spoken without thinking and the Earl remarked:

'So you have a Chef, and he is hardly, may

I point out, likely to be lurking somewhere in the basement, if there is one at Rose Cottage.'

Darcia laughed.

'Shall I tell you quite truthfully that this luncheon was prepared for me by a Chef belonging to one of my friends?'

That was true, Darcia thought, because the Chef was employed by the *Marquise*, and even though he was paid for by her father's money, she did not count him as being her personal servant.

'I was quite certain you would have an explanation,' the Earl remarked, 'but I am not sure that I believe it.'

'I cannot imagine why not.'

The Earl looked at her for a long time before he said:

'There is something about you that is exotic, although that is not the right word; that is luxurious, although you are plainly dressed; that is rich, and I am not referring to money but to your mind.'

His voice seemed to deepen as he went on:

'You do not belong to a tiny cottage and a small constricted life, because your horizons end only with the sky.'

Darcia felt herself quiver as he spoke.

Then as she did not answer because she

had no idea what to say the Earl continued:

'I want you to trust me. I dislike the secrets which exist between us. I want more than I have wanted anything for a long time for you to tell me the truth.'

'I had no idea you could be so … greedy,' Darcia said after a poignant pause.

'Greedy?' the Earl questioned.

'I offer you a Van Loo, and you want more.'

'Perhaps what I am seeking from you is more valuable than a picture.'

'Shall I suggest, so that you will not feel frustrated that there is a commode by Cressent which would look perfect in the Red Drawing-Room?'

'You are deliberately trying to side-track me,' the Earl objected, 'at the same time I know Cressent's work. He was both a sculptor and a cabinet-maker, and of course it is exactly what I need, and it will complement another commode I have in store. Mine is particularly beautiful, and the cupids are, I think, the best he ever carved.'

Darcia gave a little laugh.

'Cupids in the Dining-Room and in both Drawing-Rooms! You are certainly, My Lord, building a house filled with the symbols of love!'

The Earl unexpectedly was looking out towards the view.

'That is what I intended when I watched the first foundations being laid,' he said quietly.

There was something almost wistful in the way he spoke and Darcia without thinking said:

'You are building this house with your heart, but be careful with whom you share it!'

She knew as she spoke, that she had gone too far.

There was a frown between the Earl's eyes and he said:

'I have enjoyed a very delicious luncheon, and now I think perhaps we should go back to work, I have to drive to London later this afternoon.'

'I am ready,' Darcia replied. 'My footman will return the picnic-basket to the carriage.'

They walked back towards the house and she was aware that the Earl was still frowning.

Only when once again they began to talk of the decorations for the rooms and the colours for the curtains did the smile come back into his eyes and to his lips.

Three hours later, driving back to London Darcia felt with a mischievous little smile, that she had undoubtedly made the Earl late for dinner.

She had learned that while he was working on his house he was staying about three miles away with a friend who was delighted not only to accommodate him, but his horses.

By the time he had driven there, first to change, then to reach London, and change again into evening-clothes, he would either have to send a message to Lady Caroline saying that dinner would be later than he had intended, or keep her waiting.

The thought of Lady Caroline made her immediately curious to know more about her.

It was strange for one thing, that she was prepared to risk her reputation by doing anything so outrageous as to dine un-chaperoned at a bachelor establishment, even though she was secretly engaged to the Earl.

She had been very determined to see him tonight and listening to the inflections in her voice Darcia felt that perhaps she was more perceptive about them than she would have been if she could have watched Lady

133

Caroline at the same time.

It was almost, she thought, like being blind and having to use her sixth sense.

'I am certain,' Darcia told herself, 'Lady Caroline is not really in love with the Earl. She wants the prestige of being his wife, and perhaps too she desires him physically as a man, but that is not all there is to love.'

She was certain there was no affinity between them, not the closeness of minds which in some small degree she felt she herself had with him.

She gave a deep sigh.

He was intrigued, mystified and thrilled by her interest in his house, but she was certain it had never yet crossed his mind that she was desirable as a woman.

She found herself wondering all the time it took her to journey back to London exactly what he did feel for Lady Caroline, and she could not bear to remember what she felt when she had known the Earl was kissing her in the next room.

'You are looking a little sad, *ma petite,*' the *Marquise* said as they set out for the French Embassy. 'I think these visits to Rowley Park upset you. There is nothing more disturbing than that which tugs at the heart.'

That was the truth, Darcia thought, and

what was tugging at her heart was the thought of what the Earl was doing this evening.

Lady Caroline had been waiting for over twenty minutes when the Earl looking extremely handsome came into the Drawing-Room of his house in Berkeley Square.

He raised his guest's hand to his lips saying as he did so:

'Forgive me. I can only apologise very humbly for not having left the country sooner, as I intended to do.'

'I need not ask what kept you,' Lady Caroline replied. 'It was of course your house.'

'Our house,' the Earl corrected.

'I seem to have very little part in it.'

'That is not my fault,' he replied. 'If you only knew how I have longed to show you every development as it takes place, to tell you every new idea that comes to my mind, and to gain your approval for every stone as it is set in place.'

Lady Caroline sipped from the glass of champagne she held in her hand before she replied:

'Tonight I want to talk to you very seriously, Granby.'

'What about?' the Earl enquired.

'Ourselves.'

'It is a subject in which I have a proprietory interest.'

'I hope that is true.'

'Why should you doubt it?'

'Because as I told you this afternoon you have been neglecting me, and I do not like it!'

'Forgive me,' the Earl said again. 'As you know, I have been trying to build a perfect background for your beauty, and as soon as I have it ready you will glow in it as the greatest treasure I possess, and that is the truth.'

'That all sounds very romantic, but quite frankly, Granby, I am sick of waiting. Let us get married now, and finish your house together.'

'That would spoil everything,' the Earl protested. 'When you first told me you loved me I was determined not only to give you a monument to our love, but create a place which will be a home for us, our children and the future generations which will bear my name.'

'I am sure, as Papa has said, that is a very laudable ambition,' Lady Caroline said, 'but I want to be married now, before the Season ends.'

The Earl drew in his breath to find words to answer, but the Butler announced dinner.

It was impossible to talk intimately while the servants were in the room and the Earl told Lady Caroline about the picture he had been offered of *Venus, Mercury and Cupid.*

'I have never heard of it,' she said petulantly. 'Why does it interest you so much?'

'Because it is not only perfect for the Red Drawing-Room, but is in my opinion, one of the finest pictures painted in the last century. You must have heard of Louis Michel Van Loo?'

'I expect the name was dinned into my ears with the names of other artists when I was in the School-Room,' Lady Caroline replied, 'but all I can remember is Botticelli's *"Venus"* because so many people have said that she looks like me.'

'Or to be accurate, you look like her,' the Earl corrected.

Lady Caroline shrugged her shoulder.

'What does it matter? Why do you not buy that picture?'

The Earl laughed.

'If it were possible I can assure you I would willingly do so, but I doubt if the Italian Government would part with it even for several million pounds. I have learnt in this life it is no use crying for the moon, Caroline.'

'That is what I feel I am doing when I keep asking you to marry me.'

The servants had left the room and the Earl put his hand over hers.

'You know that I want you to be my wife.'

'Do you?'

'I have told you so often enough.'

'I prefer actions to words,' Lady Caroline said pouting in a way which most men found irresistible.

'I will find out how quickly the house can be ready.'

Lady Caroline banged her fist down on the table.

'Bother the house!' she exclaimed. 'You can marry me, and that is what should matter!'

The Earl had not finished, but she rose from the table and left the room, fighting as she walked down the corridor to control her emotions.

Lady Caroline's relatives and certainly her father's household servants could have told him she had an extremely bad temper.

She lost it quickly, but usually though it was a tempestuous storm while it lasted, it subsided as quickly as it had arisen.

But because she seldom exerted herself to control her feelings when she was at home, she was finding it difficult now not to scream at the Earl and make him aware how angry she was at his prevarication.

'I want to get married, and I will get married this summer!' she told herself.

Her blue eyes were hard, and there was a determination in the line of her chin when the Earl joined her in the Salon.

Before Darcia left for the French Embassy she had sent for Mr Curtis.

'I want you to make arrangements to have the picture by Van Loo of *Venus, Mercury and Cupid* taken from Rowley Park tomorrow morning as early as possible and left at the Earl of Kirkhampton's new house.'

She thought as she spoke that if the picture was delivered before the Earl arrived there would be no chance of his questioning those who brought it.

Mr Curtis showed no surprise at her request. He merely said:

'I think it is the picture which hangs in the blue Drawing-Room at Rowley Park?'

'Yes, that is the one.'

'I hope the Master will not mind losing it.'

'You know as well as I do, Mr Curtis, that it is unlikely my father will ever return to England. But if he does, you and I will find something just as good for the place that has been left empty.'

Mr Curtis inclined his head at the compliment.

'I think what we will do,' Darcia went on, 'is to put aside a special fund to replace anything I sell which comes from Rowley Park. You already have the cheques for the panelling and the Boucher.'

'I will open another account as you suggest, *Mademoiselle*,' Mr Curtis said.

He would have left the room, but Darcia began to speak again and he stopped.

'There is one more thing I want you to do for me,' she said. 'I want you to find out everything you can, and I mean everything, about Lady Caroline Blakeley.'

Mr Curtis scribbled the name on his notebook.

'She is the daughter of the Duke of Hull, and spends, I believe a great deal of time with Lord Arkleigh. I would like to know where they meet and when, and anyone else she appears to favour.'

'I will let you have the information as quickly as possible, *Mademoiselle*.'

Mr Curtis's eyes were entirely expression-less.

He bowed in his usual polite, half-subservient manner and went from the room.

Darcia gave a little sigh and looked at herself in one of the mirrors, wondering what the Earl would think if he could see her now.

In her elaborate Parisian gown, with its bustle which gave her the appearance of an exotic bird she looked dazzling, very sophisticated and at the same time undoubtedly alluring.

Only her eyes had something young, untouched and innocent about them.

There was also a depth which to a student of human nature would have been unmistakable – a yearning for love.

CHAPTER FIVE

Riding back to the country the next morning the Earl felt that he was escaping from something that definitely troubled him.

At the same time he was upset.

He had known when Lady Caroline dined with him last night that she had asked herself for a special purpose and was not likely to be diverted from it.

At the same time the Earl had told himself that he was not going to be pressurised into upsetting his plans or spoiling what he considered to be the perfection of them.

Ever since he had been a boy the Earl had sought perfection in everything he did.

The reason why he was such a good rider was that he not only had a natural ability to ride a horse, but also because he studied the science of it, the animals he controlled, and was always prepared to consider new ideas whenever he found them.

The same applied to his studies when he was at Oxford, and his Tutors were amazed at the manner in which he concentrated on his work despite temptations of a more frivolous nature which his contemporaries found irresistible.

When after his family mansion was burned down the Earl determined to build a new house, he not only visited the famous houses all over England and France, but he also consulted architects of both countries and collected a library on the subject.

Those who worked with him were astonished at his eye for detail.

He decided, for instance, he would import Percheron horses from Normandy because they had proved on other building operations stronger when it came to the cartage of large trees.

By the time the foundations of his house were done the Earl knew more about the future building than any of the architects, designers and contractors he had engaged.

It was when he first had the idea of building his house to his own specifications that he met Lady Caroline Blakeley and thought she was the most beautiful girl he had ever seen.

He had in fact been so busy winning races, riding horses and educating himself that he had not given much attention to women.

That they noticed and pursued him was inevitable.

He was not only exceedingly handsome, he also belonged to one of the great families of England and was acknowledged to be very wealthy.

He had however paid little attention to the ambitious mothers who thrust their offspring at him, or the wiles of married women with complacent husbands.

Actually he had two or three mild *affaires de coeur* with the latter which only came to an end when he found something else of more absorbing interest than playing the gallant in a scented *Boudoir*.

That he had a mistress went without saying, for the simple reason that it was as fashionable as having superb horses, or belonging to the best Clubs.

Here again the women to whom he offered his protection found it difficult to keep his interest, and once they had passed to some more ardent protector, the Earl found it hard even to remember their names.

With Lady Caroline he was enamoured by her beauty as he never had been before.

She seemed to him to be the epitome of perfection and that was what he required in his life, in his wife, and as the chatelaine of his perfect house, which was already taking shape within his mind.

When she accepted him it was what he expected and he settled down to build what he knew would be a unique frame for her loveliness.

Because he liked everything he did to be well organised as the result of careful, meticulous planning, he had no wish to be married with the hurry that Lady Caroline seemed to think was essential.

'I have told you,' he said when dinner was over and they were sitting in the Drawing-Room, 'that the house will be ready in four or five months. Tomorrow I will ask if the work can be accelerated, but I think it unlikely.'

He saw Caroline's lips tighten and he added:

'Already I have created a record in building such a large house so quickly.'

'Then create another by marrying me at the end of the month!'

'That would hardly be a record,' the Earl replied, 'in fact many people would consider it a show of unseemly haste.'

'You can hardly say that!' Caroline snapped at him, 'when we have been engaged for the last two years.'

'Secretly,' the Earl said. 'And we arranged that no-one should know about it except your father.'

'It is my father who wishes us now to be married.'

The Earl looked surprised.

'He has said nothing to me.'

'Papa has told me that he thinks it is time we were married, and people are asking why you are so tardy in your wooing.'

'People who say that sort of thing are not of any importance,' the Earl said quickly.

'But I presume I am,' Caroline answered. 'I want to be married. I want to be your wife.'

The Earl had risen from the sofa on which they were sitting side by side to stand with his back to the mantelpiece.

He looked extremely handsome and elegant in his evening clothes, but Caroline's blue eyes were hard as she said:

'Look what I do for you! I came here tonight so that we could be alone, risking my reputation, for you well know if anyone knew about it, what interpretation they would put on such an action.'

'It was your suggestion,' the Earl said, 'and quite frankly, Caroline, although I did not like to say so, I thought it was a mistake.'

He saw the fury in her expression, but he told himself that he should have refused to let her do anything so unconventional as to come here alone to his house in Berkeley Square.

It was the sort of behaviour which in his eyes tarnished her perfection and which he did not wish from his future wife.

Then thinking he had been a little harsh, he said in a more considerate tone:

'I am of course touched and honoured, Caroline, that you trust me. At the same time I must think for you, or if you like protect you from yourself. This must not happen again.'

'There will be no reason for it to happen, if we are married.'

Because she thought she was using the wrong tactics with him Caroline rose and moved towards him.

She put her hands on his shoulders and looked up at him, well aware that the light from the chandelier was turning her fair hair to shimmering gold.

'We must not quarrel, Granby,' she said in a soft, seductive little voice, 'I love you, and you love me, and nothing is more frustrating than that we should not be together.'

The Earl's arms went round her and he thought as she pressed herself against him that she was yielding and sweet as a woman should be.

He was just about to tell her that he loved her when Caroline's lips were on his and she kissed him with an urgency and a passion which surprised him.

The Earl was used to women being demanding where he was concerned, but again it was something that he did not find particularly attractive in the woman whom he intended to marry.

He had always treated Caroline, because she was so beautiful, as something very delicate and fragile.

He felt that she was immune from the ordinary human fiery passions until the day came when he would teach her about love with, he thought, the same expertise as he showed in everything else.

Now he was aware that Caroline was deliberately attempting to excite him and some critical part of his mind knew it was because she thought that if she did so he would agree to what she wanted.

The Earl had a very strong character and a determination which had grown at the same time as he had developed his amazing concentration.

Caroline's action made him even more determined than he had been before that he would not agree to what she wished; he felt quite simply that it would destroy the perfection he demanded for her as well as for himself.

He kissed her, or rather he submitted to the demanding insistence of her lips, but he was well aware that while she excited him as a man some idealistic part of himself was surprised almost to being shocked at the way she was behaving.

Caroline's arms went round his neck and pulled his head down closer to hers.

'Oh, Granby, Granby!' she whispered. 'How can we wait? I want to belong to you, I want to be yours. Five months will seem like five centuries if we cannot be together.'

Then before he could answer she was kissing him again, kissing him hungrily, demandingly, lighting within him a fire, but one which he knew was entirely physical.

Spiritually he stood apart and watched both himself and her.

Later when he had driven Caroline home and she had pleaded with him all the way to do what she wished, the Earl had returned to the house in Berkeley Square feeling extremely perturbed.

Because he had no wish to go on arguing over the same subject he told Caroline before he left her that he would at least consider whether it would be possible for their marriage to take place sooner than he had intended.

He had known this had given her a little hope, but even she was suspicious of it being just a device on his part to make the evening end amicably.

The Earl had however lain awake in the darkness trying not to face facts that were so unpleasant that he would have preferred to ignore them.

But they persisted and not even the freshness of the morning air and the fact that he was riding a new and spirited stallion he had only recently bought could dispel the cloud that seemed to envelop him.

Because he wished to travel quickly he took to the fields as soon as he was out of London and reached his house in record time.

As he saw its towers and chimneys silhouetted against the sky he felt once again the elation that had made every day he was building it one of joy.

The sunshine was glittering on the windows and he thought that what he had created was a dream in stone and mortar like Chenonceux.

It was certainly his dream and now it was nearly complete, but he knew he could not rest or relax until there were no longer workmen moving around the building, and the garden now obscured by the piles of building materials was as perfect as the house.

It was not quite a quarter-past-ten when he swung himself from his horse and a groom came running from the stables to lead the animal away.

As the Earl walked up the steps to the front door he was thinking, and it lifted his heart for the first time, that in another three-quarters-of-an-hour the Van Loo would be arriving from Darcia.

It was still hard to believe that it was the genuine picture that she was able to sell him and he would not find on arrival that it was fake.

Thinking of it he walked instinctively through the main Hall, through the Red Drawing-Room into the next room to which so far he had not given a name.

Then as he glanced almost casually towards the wall on which he had decided to hang the picture he saw to his astonishment that it was already there.

Propped up under the place where it would hang it was exactly as the Earl had visualised it, only even more beautiful.

He knew then as he saw the deep blue silk against which Venus was standing the name of the room and almost like a puzzle falling into place the other pictures, the furniture and the curtains.

It would be 'The Blue Room' and a very different blue from the colour of Caroline's eyes.

There was something strong and out-standing about the Van Loo picture that was different from the soft loveliness of the Boucher cupids which Darcia had brought him previously.

The Van Loo Venus standing upright in all the perfection of her nakedness made the Earl feel as if she portrayed a power of beauty and love that was the ultimate of inviolable perfection.

He stood in front of the picture taking in every detail of the contrast between Venus's white body and the bronzed, sun-burnt sheen of Mercury.

The messenger of the gods was sitting at her feet and the Earl remembered that in one of the mythological stories she had married Mercury and Cupid was their son.

As he looked at the child in the picture leaning across his father's knee to write on a piece of paper that he held for him the Earl knew that one day he would teach his own children, and especially his sons, all the things he himself had learned.

He thought that many of the rooms in his house would be filled not with distinguished guests or frivolous beauties who would demand that he spend his time complimenting or entertaining them, but with his own children.

As he thought about it he knew that there could be no more perfect place in which to bring up his family than the house he had built with its twisting staircase and its towers.

The banisters, he thought, would make a good slide, and the strange little nooks and corners were perfect for 'Hide-and-Seek'.

Outside in the stables which were now finished there would be room for numbers of ponies, for children's carriages, and of course in the winter the sleighs and toboggans when snow covered the hill on which the house was built.

It was as if everything he had been doing fell into place and he was aware more vividly than he had ever been before why this particular house was so necessary to him and why it was the fulfilment of all his needs and aspirations.

He felt almost as if after a long, long journey he had found, like Jason, the Golden Fleece for which he had been searching, and everything that had been in his heart and mind, although he had not been aware of it, was now concentrated into a whole by the picture at which he was looking.

He gave a deep sigh of satisfaction and it suddenly struck him that Venus's hair which was dark red and coiled round her head in a plait was very different from the gold of Caroline's and in fact more reminiscent of Darcia's.

He remembered noticing when they had been picnicking together under the trees how the sunlight gleaming through the leaves had touched Darcia's hair and revealed red lights which had glowed like little flames.

He had been so intent at the time on what they were saying to each other that he had not thought of it until now, but as it struck him how alluring it had been he remembered too that her eyes, which in retrospect had seemed abnormally large, were green.

The colour of the eyes of Venus in the picture could not be seen because she was looking down at Mercury, but with her red hair the Earl suspected that only green would satisfy the artistry of the painter.

'How can I thank Darcia for bringing me anything so lovely and absolutely right for this room?' he asked himself.

After standing for a long time looking at the picture he went to find his plans so that he could add to the list of items he required to be brought from where the Kirkhampton furniture was stored, exactly what he required for the Blue Drawing-Room.

Six days later Darcia was writing her letters of thanks when Mr Curtis came into the room.

As he shut the door carefully behind him she was aware he had something to tell her and knew he had chosen his moment well.

She and the *Marquise* had been to a large luncheon party and the Frenchwoman had now gone upstairs to lie down in preparation for a Ball they would attend tonight given at Marlborough House.

It was only due to the prestige of the *Marquise* that Darcia was invited for 'The Marlborough House Set', as it was called, did not as a rule include young girls.

The Prince and Princess of Wales entertained married friends of their own age or older men and women, and they were all extremely sophisticated.

'It is a very great honour for you,' the *Marquise* had said when she received the invitation, 'and an experience which I know will delight your father.'

'Papa should go instead of me,' Darcia replied.

'He would be far more delighted than you seem to be at the moment,' the *Marquise* said. 'If you are not pleased, I think I shall wash my hands of you!'

Darcia raised her eye-brows and she explained:

'I keep asking myself, *ma petite,* what it is you want out of life. I cannot remember in all the time I have lived in Paris and London a young girl who has had more success than you have had. Everybody talks of your beauty, your gowns, your charm, and yet I have the feeling that you are only giving half your attention to what is happening. Am I wrong?'

Darcia laughed.

'I do not want to answer that question.'

'Then I will answer it for you – you are in

love!' the *Marquise* said, 'and though I have racked my brains day after day, night after night, I cannot think who it is that has captured your heart.'

'Why should you think there is anyone?'

The *Marquise* made a typically French gesture with her hands.

'What debutante refuses the offers of marriage you have refused unless her interest lies elsewhere?'

The *Marquise* held up her hand and started to tick off on her fingers one after another the men who had asked Darcia to marry them.

She had only counted on three fingers before Darcia cried:

'Stop! I cannot bear to hear you talking about them. You have pressed me hard enough as it is to accept their titles, their tumbledown ancestral homes and their overdrafts.'

'That is not fair!' the *Marquise* argued. 'Lord Hilton is as rich as you are.'

Darcia shrugged.

'He made my flesh creep. I thought him horrible!'

'I have never seen anyone so in love,' the *Marquise* went on relentlessly, 'as dear D'Arcy Arlington.'

'He is much too young to marry anybody!'

'He is three years older than you are,' the *Marquise* replied, 'but you obviously prefer an older man. Who is he?'

Darcia walked restlessly across the room.

'I have not admitted to there being anyone.'

'You do not deceive me.'

'Then shall I say I do not want to talk about it?'

'Which means he has not proposed!' the *Marquise* exclaimed. '*Ma chère*, I hope you know what you are doing. These proposals, and they are very important ones, may never come again.'

Darcia did not reply. She only knew that if every man in England was on his knees in front of her except for one, she would go on waiting and hoping...

'May I talk to you for a moment, *Mademoiselle?*' Mr Curtis asked.

'Yes, of course,' Darcia replied.

She rose from the writing-desk eagerly.

She had been waiting for Mr Curtis to bring her the information she required but she had not liked to seem impatient.

'I have made very extensive enquiries as you asked me to do about Lady Caroline Blakeley,' Mr Curtis began.

'I knew you would not fail me,' Darcia said.

She sat down on a chair near the fireplace and Mr Curtis stood in front of her.

'I thought it wisest not to put anything in writing.'

'No, of course not. Tell me what you have learned.'

'I understand,' Mr Curtis said in a completely expressionless voice, 'that because Lady Caroline is continually in the company of Lord Arkleigh her father the Duke has become extremely annoyed.'

'She is in love with Lord Arkleigh?' Darcia asked.

'So I understand, *Mademoiselle*. In fact it is a love-affair which has existed for a long time.'

'Why does she not marry him, I wonder?' Darcia asked almost as if she spoke to herself.

'Lord Arkleigh is already married.'

Darcia looked startled.

'I had no idea of that.'

'His wife stays in the country with their children, and it is well known that she does not like London.'

Darcia's eyes were on Mr Curtis's face as he continued:

'The Duke is delighted that there is an understanding between the Earl of Kirk-hampton and Lady Caroline, but His Grace is afraid the arrangement may break down.'

'I am not surprised,' Darcia said, again speaking almost to herself.

'His Grace has therefore told his daughter she is to be married as soon as possible. In the meantime he has forbidden her to see Lord Arkleigh.'

'Will Lady Caroline obey him?'

'That is what I was going to speak about, *Mademoiselle,* but it is a somewhat delicate subject, and I feel uncomfortable at having to speak of it to you.'

'Tell me in the same way, Mr Curtis, that you would tell my father if he was here. He told me I could always rely on you, and it is important to me on this particular matter to know the truth.'

'Very well, *Mademoiselle,* but because His Grace has imposed a ban, and a very stringent one, on Lady Caroline seeing Lord Arkleigh, they have had, in order to do so, to behave in an unconventional and reprehensible fashion.'

'What do you mean by that?'

'There is a small Hotel which you would not know of, *Mademoiselle,* off St James's

Street, called *The Griffin* which has a reputation of being used by people in Society who do not wish to be seen.'

Darcia was listening attentively as Mr Curtis went on:

'There are private rooms available for ladies and gentlemen to dine alone together in which they can...'

Mr Curtis hesitated before he continued:

'...stay as long as they wish.'

'I understand,' Darcia said.

'There are no questions asked,' Mr Curtis continued, 'and the rooms are usually booked in an assumed name.'

'So that is where Lady Caroline meets Lord Arkleigh!'

Mr Curtis nodded.

'How often do they go there?'

'I understand it is frequently,' Mr Curtis replied, 'and dinner in a private room has been booked by a "Mr Payne" for tomorrow evening.'

Darcia drew in her breath.

'Thank you, Mr Curtis. You have told me exactly what I wanted to know, and there is one more thing I want you to do for me.'

Mr Curtis drew out his note-book and took down what Darcia required without showing a flicker of surprise on his rather lugubrious face.

The Earl had to admit that he had found himself considerably distracted from his work on the house by the fact that Darcia had not called to see if he was pleased with the picture.

It seemed incredible that she did not want to hear how delighted he was with his latest acquisition.

He found himself thinking desperately that he was losing her interest and that the house would suffer in consequence.

He was passing through the West Gallery on his way from the room which was to be his special Study where there was still a great deal to be done, when glancing casually through the window he saw coming down the drive a carriage.

There was no mistaking the sudden leap of his heart and he walked quickly to the front door and met Darcia half-way towards the house.

He held out both his hands in greeting.

'At last! Where have you been hiding? Why have you neglected me? I have been expecting you every day for what seems like a century!'

He spoke so impulsively in a manner

which was very unlike the usual way he addressed her, that Darcia felt as if her whole being came to life.

Then without even thinking about it, both her hands were in his and she felt the warm strength of his fingers and knew a happiness that was unlike anything she had ever felt before.

'I have been busy ... busy,' she faltered because she knew he expected her to say something.

'I have been wondering if I had offended you, or if I had said something inadvertently for which you were punishing me.'

'It was neither of those things.'

'Then come and see your picture. I have hung it and, as you so rightly knew, it is exactly what the room wanted.'

They walked together into the house and on into the Blue Drawing-Room.

As they entered it Darcia gave a little gasp of surprise for now not only was the picture hung in place, but the room was also furnished.

There was a carpet on the floor which matched the blue of Venus's background and the curtains with exquisitely draped pelmets were of the same colour.

The sight thrilled her because for the first

time she saw furniture in place against the pale blue walls of the room and chairs covered in *petit-point* that she knew were what she would have chosen herself, had he asked her to do so.

The Earl's eyes were on her face as she looked around, knowing without her having to say so in words how much it delighted her.

Then he said quietly:

'As you can see I have left a place for the commode by Cressent. You did promise it to me.'

'I have not forgotten.'

They smiled at each other as if they were so closely in accord that words were really unnecessary.

'When may I have it?'

It would be impossible, Darcia thought, to resist the excitement in his voice.

'Tomorrow,' she said, 'if you wish, but there is something else I have to tell you about.'

'I am sure it is something I really need.'

'Not of necessity, but I feel sure you will want it.'

'What is it?'

'It is a clock combined with a gold bird-cage which is also a musical box.'

The Earl gave a little exclamation and Darcia finished:

'It was made in Switzerland in about 1780.'

'It is something I have always wanted,' the Earl said, 'but there was nothing like that at Kirkhampton House.'

'The bird's feathers are of course, real,' Darcia went on, 'and when the music plays he opens and shuts his beak, his tail moves, and he flutters his wings.'

'It is something I want now – at this moment!'

Darcia laughed.

'You may have it this evening, but it is a little more complicated than the other things I have brought you.'

'In what way?' the Earl enquired.

'Because the present owner, a very old man, will not give it to me, but only to the person who actually buys it.'

She paused before she went on:

'This particular bird-cage clock is very precious, and he wants to tell the future owner of it exactly how to use it.'

'I see no difficulty in that,' the Earl said. 'When may I meet this gentleman?'

'He is very old and very frail,' Darcia said, 'and I am afraid he cannot come to you, but you must go to him.'

'I am only too willing to do so.'

'It will mean calling at the Hotel where he is staying in London tonight, and he suggests about ten o'clock would be a convenient time.'

'Again there is no problem.'

Darcia looked a little shy.

'I am afraid he insists I accompany you. He is always apprehensive that treasures will be acquired by people who will not appreciate them, and I have to vouch for anyone I think worthy.'

'I am in your hands,' the Earl said simply.

'I would like you to have this bird-cage,' Darcia continued. 'It is unique, and I believe it is the only one in the world of that particular model, for soon after it was completed the clock-maker died.'

'You will tell me where it is to stand in the house?' the Earl asked. 'And I am prepared to promise you and its present owner that no-one shall ever touch it except myself.'

'I think that would make him happy,' Darcia said. 'Now show me the other rooms you have completed.'

'In a minute,' the Earl said. 'If we are to be with the old gentleman at ten o'clock, where are we to meet?'

'Anywhere you wish.'

'Then I would naturally be honoured if you would dine with me.'

It flashed through the Earl's mind as he spoke that last night he had been, if not shocked, certainly surprised that Caroline was prepared to dine alone with him in Berkeley Square.

He wondered if perhaps he was doing something wrong in inviting Darcia to be his guest.

Then he told himself he was being absurd. Caroline was one thing, but a woman with whom he had a business relationship and whose name he did not even know, was very different.

He did not however, miss the perceptible hesitation before Darcia replied:

'I ... shall be delighted. I am also curious about your house in Berkeley Square.'

'It was of course my father's,' the Earl replied, 'and when I have time, which will be when I have finished this house, I intend to make quite a number of alterations. However I know that the pictures will please you.'

'I shall look forward to seeing them.'

'Then may I send a carriage for you? I usually dine at eight o'clock.'

'I will drive in my own, and leave in the same way.'

The Earl laughed.

'More mysteries? Still determined to keep up your anonymity?'

'You told me it intrigued you.'

'It does, but I also find it extremely annoying.'

'I am sorry about that.'

'I have already said that I want you to trust me. I feel we know so much about each other now, and there is no need for games or pretence.'

For a moment Darcia wondered if she should tell him the truth.

Then she asked herself how far could the truth go, and anyway it would be impossible to admit that she was the rich *Comtesse* about whom everyone in London was talking.

It would raise a very pertinent question as to why she was pretending to be in need of money, and also from where did she get the amazing treasures that had brought him such delight.

'No, no!' she told herself quickly.

Her plans had succeeded so far and she would make a great mistake if she revealed too soon her real object in seeking him out in the first place.

It was easy because they had moved into the Library to divert the Earl's attention from herself by exclaiming over the fantastically beautiful collection of pictures that were assembled there.

There was also French furniture about which she was glad she could show that she was so knowledgeable. She knew that he was surprised at how much she knew about the work of Riesener and Dubois.

The Earl took her into the Morning-Room and an amusing little Tower Drawing-Room.

Then they went back to see that the Breakfast Room was now complete with a table and chairs that were covered in Beauvais tapestry.

It was nearly half-past-twelve when Darcia said quickly:

'I must leave you. I have to get back to London.'

'Do you mean to tell me you have brought no picnic with you? I was so looking forward to another like the one we enjoyed the last time you were here.'

'I am sorry,' Darcia apologised, 'but I really cannot stay. Besides, I shall see you tonight.'

'Do not be late,' the Earl said, 'or I shall be

frantic wondering if you have disappeared again, and having no idea where I might find you.'

'I promise you I will not deprive you of the musical bird-cage clock, although I am very tempted to keep it for myself.'

'You would not dare!' the Earl said quite sharply.

Then they both laughed.

It was as she was driving back alone to London that Darcia asked herself if she was in fact, doing the right thing.

She had the uncomfortable feeling that she was playing with Fate and that Fate had an unpredictable way of having the last word.

At the same time she knew that somehow she had, if only for his sake, to extract the Earl from a trap that she knew had been set for him, if not only by Lady Caroline, by her father also.

It was quite obvious that any parent of a beautiful daughter would want a distinguished and rich husband for her and who better than the Earl of Kirkhampton?

At the same time, Darcia knew that like herself the Earl would never be content with a marriage that was not based on love.

Just as he had built his house with love, giving it his whole heart, so he would want to do the same in his marriage.

'He may never love me,' Darcia said. 'In fact after tonight he may hate me. At the same time, he will not be bound to a woman who loves another man.'

She was quite certain as she thought of it that Lady Caroline would have no intention of giving up Lord Arkleigh once she was married. In fact, it would make it easier for them to see each other and be together, because the Duke would not be interfering.

She had learnt the night when she was at Marlborough House how many love-affairs there were taking place amongst the guests.

Wives enamoured of their husbands' friends, husbands flirting with other men's wives.

She could see the look in their eyes when they danced together. She could sense it in the vibrations as they sat side by side on a sofa, outwardly behaving in a most exemplary manner, while their hearts beat in a very different fashion.

'How could I bear to live like that?' Darcia asked herself.

She knew when she married she wanted to be in love, to be with the man she loved, and to forget that any other man existed.

Because she loved the Earl she could not bear to think of him gradually growing more disillusioned, gradually becoming aware that his wife was unfaithful.

She knew it would hurt him and soil the perfection he sought in his house, his mind and his heart.

'I must save him,' she told herself, 'and that is really more important than anything else.'

CHAPTER SIX

Driving towards Berkeley Square in the uncrested carriage which Mr Curtis hired for her when she wished to be anonymous Darcia knew she was behaving outrageously.

She was well aware that it was inconceivable for a debutante to go alone to a bachelor's house and if anyone was aware of it – it would ruin her reputation.

She remembered how careful her father had been in Paris that no-one should know that she was visiting him, and she knew that he would be very angry if he was aware of what she was doing now.

At the same time she could not now back out and suddenly be conventional when her relationship with the Earl had already become different from anything she could imagine having with anyone else.

The gentlemen who danced attendance on her at the Balls and sent her flowers every morning and who professed themselves crazily in love were very careful not to offend propriety.

They knew that the *Marquise* was keeping a strict eye on their behaviour and because they genuinely wished to marry Darcia, they did not make the mistake of trying to lure her into the garden, or linger too long in an arbour or in a Conservatory.

Because she was young and inexperienced where men were concerned, she had no idea that her behaviour brought her the approval of the Dowagers and the most critical of hostesses.

But now her conscience pricked her and she knew that she should not only have refused the Earl's invitation to dine but she should also not have embarked on this particular adventure at all. But she was concentrating only on trying to save him from Lady Caroline.

She longed to pretend to herself that she did not love him.

At the same time, she was aware that her love, which had existed actually since she was a little girl, was concerned more with him than herself.

She felt she could not bear him to be like so many other men, unhappily married, restless, seeking amusement elsewhere and evoking either the scorn or the pity of his friends.

'Everything about him is so magnificent!' Darcia told herself. 'How could I watch him fail in what to everyone is the most important aspect of their life, their home.'

She found it impossible to understand how Lady Caroline did not appreciate what the Earl was doing for her in building a fairy-tale house that was undoubtedly made for lovers.

Then Darcia knew that love could not be forced or commanded, and if Lady Caroline really loved Lord Arkleigh then she could not love another man.

Since Mr Curtis had told her that Lord Arkleigh was married, Darcia could understand why the Duke was pressing for his daughter's marriage to the Earl to take place immediately, and was using all his parental authority to keep the lovers apart.

It was the sort of situation that to Darcia held an echo of her own life with her father.

Only then it was he who was pursuing some beautiful woman in the face of objections either from her father or her husband, and finding it all a light-hearted adventure regardless of who was hurt in the process.

'It is really very wrong,' Darcia thought, and knew that what she wanted in life was the security of a home, children and of course a husband.

When she thought of this she drew in her breath, knowing the only husband who could possibly make her happy would be the Earl.

The carriage stopped outside the Kirkhampton House and when the footman opened the door she stepped out very quickly, hurrying up the steps and into the Hall, afraid she might be seen by some passer-by.

She had taken the precaution of wearing a dark cloak over her gown to make herself less conspicuous and had covered her hair with its red lights, with a deep blue chiffon scarf which was the colour of the blue in the Van Loo picture which now hung in the Earl's Blue Drawing-Room.

As if he could not wait for her to be announced, the moment she came through the front door into the Hall he emerged from the Drawing-Room and walked towards her with a smile, his eyes taking in her appearance, especially the colour of her scarf.

There was a footman to take Darcia's cloak from her, but the Earl did it himself, and as she lifted the scarf carefully so as not to disturb the curls elegantly arranged at the back of her head, he said:

'I was half-afraid you would fail to arrive at the last moment.'

'But as you see I am here,' Darcia replied and she could not help the lilt of joy in her voice.

They went into the Drawing-Room and the Earl said:

'This is the first time I have seen you really fashionably gowned, and I might have known it would become you.'

Darcia had, in fact, hesitated for a long time as to what she should wear.

Because she was pretending that Rose Cottage was her home, and because at first she had wished him to think her a professional dealer in pictures and furniture, she had thought her plain school-gowns were appropriate.

Tonight she had rebelled against her own common sense and had stood for a long time looking at the fantastic collection of gowns she had bought in Paris.

Many of them she dismissed at first glance knowing they were suitable enough for a Ballroom, but there were others that were a little more simple, but at the same time had the undoubted *chic* and elegance of Paris

177

written all over them.

Finally she chose one which was white which was all the *Marquise* would let her wear as a debutante, but the exquisite and expensive lace with which it was trimmed was threaded through with narrow velvet ribbon in the same blue which had delighted the Earl in the Van Loo picture.

The gown revealed the smallness of her waist and the tight bodice the soft curves of her figure.

Her shoulders were bare, emerging from a froth of lace, and she wore no jewellery.

To wear jewellery, she knew, would have been a mistake; for although her father had given her a great many valuable gems, and she also had some magnificent pieces which had belonged to her mother, Darcia did not wish to make the Earl more curious than he was already.

She therefore wore only a piece of ribbon around her throat in the same velvet which decorated her gown and hanging from the front of it a tiny, exquisitely painted miniature of her mother.

Its only ornamentation was the enamel set with small diamonds which encircled the frame, while the miniature itself was a masterpiece.

As she might have expected the Earl's eyes were attracted to it automatically.

'I have never seen a miniature more beautifully displayed,' he said as he handed her a glass of champagne.

Instinctively she put her free hand up to her throat.

'Do you mean the frame?' she asked innocently.

'I was referring to its position on your neck,' he replied.

To her annoyance she blushed because she was not used to compliments from him and he said:

'I do not need to tell you that your appearance is perfection, as is everything else you do.'

Because she felt a little shy Darcia looked around the room.

'Here are the pictures I have longed to see!' she exclaimed.

'Why do you not say you longed to see me?' the Earl enquired. 'As you well know you have neglected me shamefully, and I expect you to make reparation by being particularly kind to me tonight.'

'I hope to do that by delighting you with the musical bird-cage.'

'Everything in its right place at its right

time,' the Earl said. 'I am content for the moment to be delighted with you.'

Darcia was rather surprised.

She felt he was speaking to her in a different way from what he had ever done before.

Then she told herself it was because they were not thinking only of the house he was building, but were in fact just a man and a woman having dinner together, and they could therefore be interested in each other.

Dinner was announced and Darcia looking round the Dining-Room saw it had a formal appearance except for the pictures, which all by 18th century masters were superb.

'I would like to show you some very lovely Gainsboroughs which I have in another room,' the Earl said, 'but we must not linger here too long, or your friend might not wait.'

'No, indeed,' Darcia agreed.

Because she wanted to please him she turned the conversation to horses and knew that while the Earl was obsessed at the moment with the building of his house his first love had by no means paled into insignificance.

Because her father had always owned race-horses in almost every country in which he stayed for any length of time, Darcia knew a great deal about breeding and training and the Earl was surprised by her knowledge.

'How can you know so much about a subject that is not yours?' he asked.

'As I said to you the first time you showed me your view, one does not actually have to own something to possess it.'

'I understand,' he said, 'because it is what I have always felt myself.'

He paused for a moment before he added:

'Somebody the other day asked me why I did not buy Botticelli's *"Venus"*, but because every time I visit Florence I go to look at it, I feel it is mine.'

'I felt the same thing.'

'You have been to Florence?' he exclaimed in surprise.

'Some years ago.'

She remembered as she spoke the Villa her father had owned outside Florence until he grew bored with it and the beautiful Florentine lady who had amused him until he grew bored with her too.

'Is love always so short-lived?' Darcia asked herself suddenly.

'You are looking wistful,' the Earl said unexpectedly, 'an expression I have never seen on your face before.'

'How do you know that is what I am feeling?'

'Your eyes are very expressive, Darcia,' he replied, 'and you know that we do not always have to explain things to each other in words.'

'No, that is true.'

'I understand a great deal about you,' he went on, 'and that is why I find it so frustrating when there is a barrier I cannot demolish and you will not trust me.'

Darcia smiled at him. 'Perhaps one day.'

'I hate half-promises,' the Earl said sharply, 'just as I dislike the fact that I am never sure when I will see you again.'

'I always turn up like the proverbial bad penny,' Darcia replied lightly.

'That is a most inappropriate simile,' the Earl objected. 'You are more like a light shining in the darkness, or perhaps a star glittering in the night sky. Your eyes arouse my ambitions and aspirations.'

'Do they really make you feel like that?' Darcia asked teasingly.

'Not so long ago I should have answered no to that question,' the Earl said. 'Now when I know you, the answer is yes.'

There was something in the way he spoke which made her feel a little breathless, as if her heart turned over in her breast.

Then because there was so much to say, so much to laugh about, dinner was quickly over, and because they were in a hurry there was no time to see the pictures in the other rooms, as they had to leave for their appointment at ten o'clock.

'We will go in my carriage, if you please,' Darcia said and the Earl did not argue.

Her cloak was waiting for her in the Hall and once again she covered her hair with the blue chiffon scarf and wound it round her neck.

The Earl thought she looked like Romney's picture of the beautiful Lady Hamilton, but he did not say so, only followed her across the pavement and into the comfortable carriage.

'Where are we going?' he asked as the horses started to move round the Square in the direction of Berkeley Street.

'*The Golden Griffin,*' Darcia replied.

The Earl stiffened.

'*The Golden Griffin?*' he repeated almost incredulously. 'That is certainly not the sort of place to which I should take you!'

'If we are truthful, it is I who am taking you!' Darcia corrected. 'It is where Mr Quincey is staying and has, I believe, stayed every time he visits London from the country for the last twenty-five years.'

She thought the Earl shrugged his shoulders, but he said no more, and when they drew outside *The Golden Griffin* Darcia looked at it a little apprehensively.

It certainly seemed quiet and unobtrusive.

There was nothing significant about the vestibule, and Darcia went to the Reception Desk to ask for Mr Quincey.

She had been thankful as she entered *The Golden Griffin* that there was nobody in sight except for the Hotel servants.

But once again she knew that if the *Comtesse* de Sauze was seen in a place with such a dubious reputation it was an indiscretion that would undoubtedly be circulated around Mayfair by the following morning.

The Clerk at the Reception desk merely bowed politely in response to her request and replied:

'Mr Quincey is expecting you, Ma'am.'

He handed her a card on which was written the number of a room and carrying it in her hand Darcia moved quickly towards the stairs followed by the Earl.

She was also carrying something else, a small package wrapped up in soft paper and tied with a bow of ribbon.

She had taken it from the opposite seat of the carriage as they had turned into St James's Street.

'What is that?' the Earl had enquired.

'It is a present I have for Mr Quincey.'

'Let me carry it for you.'

'It is very fragile,' she replied, 'and so I prefer not to trust it to anyone but myself.'

'I consider that an insult,' the Earl said. 'When I show you the china I intend to arrange in my house, some of which is pink Sèvres, I will make you apologise for the aspersions you are casting at this moment.'

'Pink Sèvres!' Darcia exclaimed with excitement. 'Do you really own some?'

'Not a lot, as it happens,' the Earl replied. 'It was in fact given to one of my ancestors by Madame de Pompadour herself!'

Darcia gave a little sigh of appreciation that was more expressive than any words.

She wished as they went up the stairs that she could give the Earl the bird-cage clock and watch his pleasure at the sight of it without having to be involved with the secrecy and subterfuge of saving him from Lady Caroline.

They reached the top of the stairs and walked along an ill-lit corridor before Darcia stopped.

She glanced at the card she held in her hand as if it was difficult to read before she said:

'Number 13. This is the room. Do not knock. Walk straight in.'

She stood back as she spoke and the Earl turned the handle of the door.

Then as he opened it, it was easy to see the whole room as if it was a stage set.

There was a table at which two people had dined almost in the centre of it, and beyond there was a wide low couch covered with silk cushions on which two people were embracing.

As the door opened they started and turned their faces towards the intruder.

Darcia had a quick glimpse of Lord Arkleigh who, having discarded his evening-coat, was in his shirt-sleeves and Lady Caroline, dishevelled but very beautiful, was in his arms.

She did not stop to look, she only walked quickly on down the corridor aware that the Earl was still standing in the doorway as if turned to stone.

Only as she reached the end of the corridor where it turned, did he catch up with her.

'I am sorry,' Darcia said before he could

speak, 'I realise now the number of the room is fifteen. It is not well written and the corridor is badly lit.'

They were already outside the door marked 15, and there was no reason for the Earl to reply, but she knew without looking at him that he was scowling, and his lips were set in a hard line.

She did not wait for him to open the door, but opened it herself. Mr Curtis was standing just inside.

'Good-evening, Miss,' he said in the polite tone of a senior servant. 'Mr Quincey is looking forward to seeing you, but I hope you will not stay long. He is not well to-day, and the doctor insists he should rest.'

'We will not keep him a moment more than necessary,' Darcia replied and walked further into the room.

Seated at the far end was a very old man in an armchair, his legs covered by a rug.

The light was not on his face, but on the table beside him on which stood what the Earl was expecting to see.

As he followed Darcia towards it he knew it was even more lovely than he had expected.

The skill with which the cage had been modelled, the intricate lacquer of the base in beautiful colours and the bird itself, could only have been fashioned by a master-hand.

'I am sorry you are not well, dear Mr Quincey,' Darcia was saying softly.

'It is … old age,' replied a quavering voice. 'It comes to all of us – but you will have to wait for a – long time yet.'

'We must not tire you,' Darcia said. 'I have brought the Earl of Kirkhampton with me. May I show him how your beautiful box works?'

'You show him, my dear,' the old man replied, 'my hands are too – shaky today.'

A key was lying on the table beside the cage, Darcia inserted it, and instantly there was music, sweet and melodious, which sounded very like the song of a bird.

Inside the gilded cage a little bird with its turquoise and crimson feathers opened and shut its yellow beak, turned round and round on its perch, fluttering its tail until just before the music ended its wings spread out to their full span, and one saw the full glory of its plumage.

Then as the last note ended the bird which really seemed to have come to life, was still.

'It is magnificent! Quite magnificent!' the Earl exclaimed.

He turned towards Mr Quincey to say:

'How can I thank you, Sir, for allowing me to have…'

He looked at the old man as he spoke and realised he was asleep.

'He is very old,' Darcia said in a whisper. 'If you put your cheque on the table he will find it when he wakes.'

The Earl drew a cheque from the inside pocket of his coat and laid it as she suggested on the table.

'Will you carry the cage,' Darcia asked, 'and do not forget the key.'

The Earl put the key in his pocket and picked up the bird-cage and Darcia laid the present she had brought for Mr Quincey down beside the envelope.

They moved quietly across the room to where Mr Curtis was waiting by the door.

'When your Master wakes,' the Earl said, 'will you tell him how very grateful I am and promise him that I will look after this treasure in the same way as he would do himself.'

'I will give him your message, My Lord.'

'Thank you,' Darcia said, as she passed Mr Curtis and they were both aware for how much she was thanking him.

They returned down the dark corridor and Darcia saw with relief that all the doors were shut including that of No. 13.

There was no-one in the vestibule and the carriage was waiting for them outside the door.

They drove away and Darcia asked:

'You are pleased?'

'That is an inadequate word to describe what I feel,' the Earl said, holding the birdcage on his knee. 'This is something unique, something I admit to never having seen before.'

'I like to think it is the Blue Bird of Happiness that you will be installing in your house.'

'It is of course the Blue Bird we all seek,' the Earl agreed. 'I did not think of that until this moment.'

'Its rightful place should be in the Blue Drawing-Room,' Darcia said, 'but do you know where I would like to put it?'

'I am waiting to hear that,' the Earl replied.

'In your special room, and if it hangs from the ceiling in front of the mirror which you have already placed over the mantelpiece you could see it reflected and re-reflected a thousand times into eternity.'

The Earl sighed for a moment, then he said:

'I can hardly bear to say this, but when I saw it standing on the table there was already a picture in my mind of where it should hang.'

'We think alike.'

'In so many ways.'

The horses drew up outside his front door and as they did so, Darcia said:

'Good-night, My Lord. I shall think of the little bird singing to you before you go to sleep.'

'There is something I wish to say before you leave,' the Earl replied, 'and I would also like you to show me once again exactly how the key works. If I should do anything wrong I would never forgive myself.'

'I will show you,' Darcia replied.

Once again she hurried into the Earl's house and they went into the Drawing-Room where he set the cage down very carefully on an inlaid table in front of the window.

He stood back to admire it saying as he did so:

'I shall never have a moment's peace until it is hanging out of reach of careless hands. Supposing a house-maid while admiring it, should knock it over?'

'It has survived for over a hundred years,' Darcia said consolingly, 'I do not believe anything will happen to it now.'

'You are tempting Fate,' the Earl said.

Darcia had taken off her cloak and chiffon scarf when she came into the hall and now the light from the candles in gold lily-lights on either side of the mantelpiece picked out the red in her hair.

While they had been away the gas-lamps had been extinguished and the room was less brilliant, but more intimate.

Darcia stood looking around her and the Earl came towards her, his eyes on her face.

'I want to thank you, Darcia,' he said, 'not only for the Blue Bird that you have found for me, but also the happiness you have given me in so many other ways.'

He put his arms around her as he spoke and when he pulled her crushingly against him he kissed her fiercely and demandingly with a violence she had somehow not expected.

Then as she realised he was angry about Lady Caroline, his lips, hard and demanding though they were, evoked in her a feeling which made her forget everything but the rapture that rose within her because she was being kissed by the man she loved.

Darcia had never been kissed before and she had imagined it was something very gentle, very seductive.

She had not thought it would be tempestuous and overwhelming, and at the same time ecstasy.

She felt the Earl's arms tighten to pull her closer and still closer until their bodies were joined almost as if they were one, and she could feel her heart beating against his and knew that he drew it from between her lips and made it his.

She was a part of him, she belonged to him, she was no longer herself but his, as she had wanted to be. It was not something she gave, but what he took, and she no longer had any will of her own but was subservient to his.

This was the love she had sought and longed for, the love that she had fought and intrigued to get, and yet now the victory was hers she was unprepared and it had come sooner than she had expected.

She had not imagined the wild joy and wonder that seemed to sweep through her and carry her away into a world that had no touch with reality, a world in which there was only the Earl, his arms, his lips and a love that was like a burning fire consuming them both.

The Earl raised his head.

'I love you, and I want you!' he said, and his voice was low and deep with passion.

'And … I love … you!'

Darcia could hardly breathe the words, and yet she felt as if she uttered them not only with her lips but with every part of her.

'You are so beautiful!' the Earl exclaimed, 'and you are my Venus – mine as surely as if I could hang you on the wall and make it the shrine you deserve.'

He kissed her again until Darcia felt she could no longer think, but only feel, and a fire that had been in his heart had now burned its way into her mind.

The Earl freed her for a moment to draw her to the sofa and they sat down as if their legs could no longer support them. Then his arms went around her to draw her against him.

'We must make plans,' he said. 'I will build you a house near me on the estate and it shall be as perfect and beautiful as the cage which holds our Blue Bird.'

'A … house?'

Darcia would have asked the question but her lips parted and there was no sound.

'In the meantime we will find somewhere where we can be together,' the Earl went on. 'Your cottage, my precious, is too small, besides which the villagers always talk. But it seems as if Fate has already played into our hands.'

Darcia put her head against his shoulder looking up at him. She felt for a moment as if she was too bemused by his kisses to understand what he was saying.

'The friend with whom I have been staying told me today that he is leaving for Scotland,' the Earl continued, 'and that if I had not been with him, he had intended to shut the house. I naturally offered to pay all expenses until my own house is ready, which will not be long. He agreed, and that, my darling, is where we will be together!'

He kissed her hair before he said:

'No-one will know where you are, and we will leave strict instructions if anyone calls that we are not at home, which will be true for most of the time, as we shall be at my house finding new ways to make it as perfect as we want it to be.'

The Earl's lips were now against the softness of her forehead before he said:

'Can you imagine how wonderful it will be if you can be with me without disappearing in that unaccountable fashion and leaving me uncertain as to when I shall see you again?'

He turned Darcia's face up to his and once again his lips were on hers, kissing her insistently, demandingly, still with a passion that left her breathless.

'I love you!' the Earl said after he had kissed her for a long time. 'I love you as I must have done from the first moment I saw you.'

He pulled her close to him as he said:

'Leave everything to me, my precious, and I will never let you have any regrets, and when we part, which I think will not be for a thousand years, I promise you that there will be no reason for you to have to engage in any more business transactions or want for money for the rest of your life.'

Darcia made a little sound, but before she could speak, before it was possible for her to say anything, the Earl's mouth held hers captive and there was nothing she could do except know the fire within him was like the heart of the sun.

Hurrying home alone an hour later Darcia lay back limply against the cushions of the carriage feeling as if it was impossible to think, impossible to realise what had happened.

When she had realised that the Earl was

offering her his protection and not marriage, she had not been shocked, only stunned by her own stupidity in not understanding that after the way she had behaved such a suggestion was inevitable.

Despite her father's raffish behaviour, she had always known that marriage between aristocratic families was something they looked on very differently from those whose blood was not blue and whose history did not go back into antiquity.

Love was not an important factor in marriage where it concerned aristocrats.

What was important was the continuance of the line and that like should mate with like, bringing into the union, if possible, advantages in the shape of land or money.

Darcia saw now how incredibly foolish she had been in thinking that in getting to know the Earl and attracting him as she had done, meant that he would want her to be his wife.

She had thought her plan was so clever and that the result would justify the means.

She had worked it all out in the same manner that the Earl had worked out the plans of his new house.

Darcia intended to surprise him first of all with her youth and beauty, then with her knowledge of the sort of pictures and furniture she knew he would need, and finally with her ability to provide them.

Everything had worked, everything had gone exactly as she wished.

She had even eliminated Lady Caroline from the competition, but even as she passed the winning-post she knew she had been disqualified from the prize entirely through her own stupidity.

'How could I not have remembered that he would never with his desire for perfection marry a woman who does not move in the same social world as he does himself?' she asked.

Then she knew despairingly that because of what he called the 'barrier' that lay between them, even if she told him now who she really was, the situation would remain unchanged.

Her father's reputation would preclude her from becoming the wife of the Earl of Kirkhampton, just as effectively as he assumed that 'Miss Darcia' who was nobody from nowhere, could be no more than his mistress.

'Papa could have explained all this to me had I asked him,' Darcia told herself.

But she knew that her father would have laughed at her and thought her childish to imagine for one moment that her wild schemes could succeed.

'He loves me as I love him,' Darcia said almost as though she was defending herself.

She knew that was not quite true. She loved the Earl so that all she wanted in life was to be his wife and the mother of his children, while the Earl desired her as a woman, but that was all.

When she reached her house she slipped quickly upstairs to her own bedroom knowing that the *Marquise* would not have returned.

As if once again Fate was making it easy for her, she had found tonight when she planned to take the Earl to *'The Golden Griffin'* that she and the *Marquise* were supposed to dine with Lord Sullivan, a very old friend and admirer of the latter.

'I have a headache,' Darcia had told the *Marquise*, 'so please make my apologies and let me go to bed.'

'I could of course cancel the dinner-party for both of us,' the *Marquise* suggested.

'That would be very foolish,' Darcia answered. 'You know as well as I do that Lord Sullivan only asked me because he wanted to see you. Please go and enjoy yourself, or you will make me feel guilty and I shall have to struggle there whether I wish to or not.'

'You have done too much today,' the *Marquise* replied, 'and *ma chère*, I do beg of you not to keep going to Rowley Park. Looking back into the past is always upsetting, and of course very tiring.'

She sounded so sympathetic that Darcia had kissed her cheek.

'Go and enjoy yourself with the man who admires you. I am quite certain neither of you will miss me.'

'He has a party for us,' the *Marquise* replied.

'I expect they are all his age and yours rather than mine,' Darcia said, 'and after a quiet night I shall look my best for the Duchess of Newcastle's Ball, which she intends to make the most brilliant of the Season.'

The *Marquise* was mollified.

'Perhaps you are wise,' she admitted. 'There is nothing more tiresome than trying to be bright and amusing when one's head is throbbing.'

As the *Marquise* had been invited for half-past-seven, it was easy for Darcia to wait until she had left the house, then drive to Berkeley Square.

Now she knew that, admonished by Mr

Curtis as to what they should and should not say, no-one in the household would reveal that she had been anywhere that evening except in her own bed.

It was only when she was undressed and her maid had left her that Darcia lay staring helplessly in the darkness, every nerve in her body throbbing still from the emotions the Earl had aroused in her.

For the moment she could not think of the future.

All she could think of was that she loved him not only whole-heartedly as she had thought before she went to dine with him tonight, but with a passion and a violence that was equal to his.

That was one side of her love, but Darcia knew that hers had something which the Earl's lacked: a spiritual awareness that they were one, and that neither time nor convention, nor any laws or restrictions invented by man could ever separate them.

'I belong to him,' Darcia thought, 'but in this life, because of the barriers that exist between us, we can never be together.'

It was one thing to think philosophically and believe in reincarnation, and quite another to know that in the years ahead she would be lonely and desperately, miserably unhappy if she could not be with the Earl, and the only way she could be was to do as he asked.

She could accept his protection, even though it meant she would become a social *pariah* for the rest of her life.

Even as she thought it she knew it was impossible, not only because it would hurt her father, but also because she knew in her heart of hearts that it would destroy the perfection of her love whatever it might do to the love the Earl had for her.

'If he loves perfection in his house,' Darcia reasoned, 'then I want perfection from him. I want him as my husband. I want to keep him loving me so that no other woman will ever mean anything in his life. I want my children to play in the house he has just built, to ride the ponies he said he would keep in the stables, and to grow up reflecting a part of his character and mine.'

That was the real meaning, she knew, when together a man and a woman made one perfect person, and that was something which now she would never find.

'It is my own fault … entirely my own … fault,' she told herself.

But it was too late to do anything about it.

The Earl had been so intent on telling her

what he wanted to arrange for them that he did not notice that she was unaccountably quiet.

It would in fact have been difficult for her to speak because when he was not talking he was kissing her, and she knew the first violence of his kisses which had been partly because he was angry had now changed to a fiery desire which swept away the thought of everything else, including the perfidy of Lady Caroline.

His whole mind, his whole interest was now concentrated on deciding their future and how they could be together.

'When will you come to me, my precious?' he had asked when finally Darcia managed to say that she must leave.

'I will … think about … it,' she answered.

'Do you imagine that is the answer I want to hear?' the Earl asked. 'I have told you I cannot wait. I want you now, tomorrow, the next day, and it will drive me crazy if you disappear again, or keep me working alone in the house when we might be together.'

He spoke in a manner which told her that what he said was utterly sincere, but it had in fact not struck him for one moment that he might offer her the position so recently vacated by Lady Caroline.

'My friend leaves tomorrow,' he said insistently. 'Will you come to me on Friday?'

She did not answer and his lips were very near to hers as he said:

'Promise me, promise me, so that I will have something to look forward to! Oh, my darling, we will be so happy!'

As if the mere idea of such happiness excited him he kissed until she put up her hands defensively and gave a little cry of protest.

'Please ... you are ... frightening me!'

Instantly he became more gentle.

'Forgive me, my sweet, but you excite me to madness! It is something which according to mythology goddesses did very skilfully when they condescended to mere mortals.'

'At the moment ... I am ... mortal too,' Darcia said in a soft voice.

'I know that, and I cannot tell you how much it thrills me.'

He looked down at her green eyes staring up into his and said:

'I cannot believe, and yet I have to ask you the question, has there ever been another man in your life?'

'No-one!' Darcia whispered.

'That is what I thought,' the Earl said

triumphantly, 'and you have never been kissed?'

'No … never!'

'It seems impossible! It makes me feel I am the luckiest, most fortunate man in the world!'

He kissed her again more gently, then he said:

'I will not frighten you, my precious little love. I will remember that like my Blue Bird you have to be handled with care. But I will teach you to sing only with me, and our love will be so beautiful that we will attain a perfection that is known only to the gods.'

When he spoke like that Darcia thought that she could not be happier if he put a dozen wedding-rings on her fingers.

Then she knew that however glorious it sounded it was not what she really wanted.

She had torn herself away from him, still leaving the question unanswered as to when she was to come to him, still up until the last moment refusing to tell him who she was.

'Why must you be so secretive?' he asked. 'Now that you belong to me there is no need for it.'

'I am not yet yours.'

'But you will be,' he said, 'and that by the way is a vow. Now that I know you love me, nothing could ever come between us.'

They had reached the door but before he opened it he kissed her until the room whirled around her and it was hard to walk across the hall and down the steps into her carriage.

Now the rapture and wonder of those kisses seemed to mock her in the darkness.

'This is the end!' her mind told her. 'Tomorrow, the next day and the day after he will wait for you at the house in vain. But he is not likely to find you, for he will not attend any social functions for fear of meeting Lady Caroline.'

Darcia was uncomfortably aware that she would always be afraid of seeing him and because she loved him his face would always be before her eyes, and his strong, athletic body would haunt her dreams.

'I love him! I love him!' she thought despairingly, 'and there is nothing I can do except when the Season ends to leave England and never come back.'

She knew in fact that was what she would have to do. It would be impossible to live so close to the Earl, and yet not see him.

She had the frightening feeling that despite all her principles and her ideals she might go to him simply because her need was so great.

Then she would be no better than Lady Caroline, and perhaps worse.

Her whole training and education, her intellectual powers by which she had reasoned out a way of life long before she came to London, told her in no uncertain terms what was right, not only according to God, but also psychologically.

She was clever enough to be aware that love to be real must contain respect and that was one thing she would never have from the Earl as his mistress.

'It is over ... finished!' Darcia said in a whisper.

Then the tears came – slow, scalding, and very painful.

CHAPTER SEVEN

Darcia felt she had only been asleep for a few minutes when she was awakened by a knock on the door.

She opened her eyes knowing she had not slept before dawn, and her head was aching from sheer tiredness.

Her maid entered the room and came to her side.

'There's a telegram, *Mademoiselle*,' she said. 'Mr Curtis opened it, and as it's urgent thought you should have it immediate.'

'A telegram!' Darcia exclaimed wondering who it could be from.

She sat up in bed, took the telegram from the silver salver and the maid hurried across the room to pull back the curtains.

Darcia opened the telegram and looked at it only to stare in disbelief at the paper as she read:

'*Master gravely injured. Please come immediately Villa Vesta, Rome.*

Briggs.'

Darcia made a stifled cry, then she jumped

out of bed and ran along the passage to where the *Marquise* was sleeping…

Three hours later they were both travelling in the boat-train which left Victoria Station at 9.30 a.m. for Dover.

'What can have happened? How can Papa be injured?' Darcia asked the *Marquise* over and over again.

Neither of them could think of any reasonable explanation.

The maids had hurriedly packed a few things for them, but they had been concerned only with getting dressed and starting on their journey which they were both aware would take time.

As usual Mr Curtis was invaluable.

He got in touch with a Courier who was well known for his efficiency and by the time Darcia and the *Marquise* were ready the tickets had already been taken and a private carriage on the train booked for them.

The Courier then went ahead to get them a cabin in which to cross the Channel and make sure they had the best accommodation available on the train which would carry them through France and into Italy.

'I am sure Mr Turnbull who will be travelling with you from Dover, *Mademoiselle*,' Mr

Curtis said to Darcia, 'will look after you as the Master would wish.'

'Briggs would not have sent for me unless it was serious,' Darcia said in a low voice.

'I hope by the time you arrive, *Mademoiselle,* nothing will be as bad as you anticipate,' Mr Curtis answered quietly.

She felt because he was fond of her father that he was praying as she was that with his proverbial good luck Lord Rowley would rally and survive any injuries he had sustained.

Then, as if she suddenly remembered what had happened last night Darcia drew Mr Curtis aside so that they could not be overheard and asked:

'You have paid the actor who played the part of Mr Quincey?'

'He was very grateful, *Mademoiselle,* for what he received.'

'He did it well.'

Darcia would have said more, but the *Marquise* called her from the door saying that it was time for them to leave and they hurried into the carriage and were driven off to the station.

Afterwards Darcia could remember very little of the long, exhausting journey which eventually took them to Rome.

All she could recall was her anxiety for her father which seemed to grow in intensity with every mile they travelled, and an ache for the Earl which became a poignant pain.

She knew that in summoning her from England Fate had once again taken a hand, and she had decided before she had to make the effort that she must go out of his life for ever.

'I will never see him again,' she thought miserably, 'and never see his finished masterpiece of a house.'

She tortured herself by imagining that when she did not come to him as he expected, he would be at first upset, then perhaps angry.

It was inevitable that later he would put her out of his mind and only perhaps sometimes when he looked at the caged Blue Bird and *Venus, Mercury and Cupid'* in the Blue Drawing-Room would he remember her.

Then when he had a wife to sit with him in the panelled Breakfast-Room and to use the wardrobe room next to the Master Suite, she would no longer even be a ghost to haunt him.

Something within Darcia cried out frantically that she had left her only hope of happiness behind in England, and it would have been far better if she had never met the Earl.

But what was done was done and there was no putting back the clock. Somehow, although for the moment she could not think now, she had to live her life without him.

Perhaps, she told herself, now that her father was suffering he would need her and would let her stay with him.

She decided that he would let her do that only if she told him the truth of what had happened.

He might be angry, but he would understand that it would be useless for him to have any more social ambitions on her behalf since she would never marry any man she did not love.

But she knew as if it was written in letters of fire that she could never love any man as she loved the Earl.

By the time they reached Rome Darcia was very pale after her sleepless nights and the heat of the carriage in which they had travelled.

Mr Turnbull did everything possible for their comfort, but nothing could change the weather or the fact that it was a very long journey to undertake without stopping on the way.

At last they were in Rome and the sun was shining blindingly over the Eternal City, turning the dome of St Peter's to gold and the Tiber to shimmering silver.

The carriage drawn by four magnificent horses such as her father invariably owned was waiting for them at the railway-station to carry them at a tremendous pace out of the city, up the hill until they reached the Villa Vesta.

Dazzlingly white, architecturally impressive, it was, Darcia thought, one of the most spectacular houses her father owned anywhere in the world.

She had not visited it for eight years, and then she had been thrilled by the contrast of the white building against the dark cypress trees pointing towards the sky, like sentinels and the brilliant flowers which filled the garden.

But for the moment she could think of nothing save her father and almost before the carriage stopped she had jumped out of it, to find Briggs waiting for her on the doorstep.

'How is Papa?'

Darcia could hardly ask the question, she

was so frightened.

'He's alive, Miss Darcia,' Briggs replied, 'and asking for you.'

She glanced back to see that the *Marquise* was following them and Briggs led the way up the broad stairway from the cool Hall.

'What happened?' Darcia enquired.

'He was stabbed, Miss Darcia. Stabbed by two assassins hired by an Italian nobleman who was not man enough to challenge your father himself.'

Darcia gave an exclamation of sheer horror.

She knew only too well the reason why her father had been stabbed and the jealousy which had struck him down.

Ever since she could remember there had been husbands and lovers who had hated him because of his success with their women.

She could recall his fighting at least half-a-dozen duels, and on one occasion when she was quite young challenging his opponent with bare fists, in true pugilist style, to emerge from the contest somewhat battered, but undoubtedly the victor.

But this had been a cowardly and unsporting attack, and she knew her father would resent it not only because he was injured, but because it was not the way a gentleman settled his differences.

They had reached the top of the stairs and as they were moving along the landing Darcia asked in a low voice:

'How bad is he?'

Briggs had already reached the door which Darcia knew led into her father's bedroom, but he stopped and when she saw the expression in his eyes she knew the answer before he spoke.

'I'm afraid there's no hope, Miss Darcia. He's just been hanging on because he wanted to see you.'

Before Darcia could reply Briggs had opened the door and she went into the bedroom knowing that the *Marquise* had not followed her any further.

The sun-blinds shaded the light from the windows and the room was dim as she moved across it to the magnificent carved bed which had once graced one of the Royal Palaces.

As she reached it a Nun who had been sitting at her father's bedside and who Darcia knew must have come from one of the nursing orders moved away without speaking.

'Papa!'

Darcia spoke little above a whisper, but Lord Rowley heard her and turned his head.

He was very pale, but he still looked amazingly handsome and had not lost that raffish look that women had always found irresistible.

'D – Darcia!'

His voice was little more than a croak.

He opened his hand that lay on the sheet and she slipped hers into it.

'Darling Papa, I came as quickly as I could.'

She bent forward and kissed his cheek and found his skin was cold almost as if life had already left it.

'I – wanted to – see you,' Lord Rowley said with difficulty.

'I am here,' Darcia said, 'but please, Papa, get well. I cannot lose you now.'

'It is better to – die when life is still – amusing – than to grow – old and – useless.'

'But I want you to ... stay with me!' Darcia protested. 'If you ... die, Papa ... I shall be ... alone.'

Her father closed his eyes but she could feel his hand still holding hers lightly. After a moment he said:

'Have you – found someone – to love?'

Darcia drew in her breath and for the moment she wanted to tell him the truth; that she had loved and lost. Then she knew it would upset him so she merely answered:

'Yes, Papa. I love someone very deeply in the same way you loved Mama.'

There was a smile on Lord Rowley's lips before he managed to say:

'Who – is – it?'

'It is the Earl of Kirkhampton. Do you remember? He stayed with us when I was a little girl, and I came down to the Dining-Room to kiss you good-night.'

'A good – rider. I am – glad – poppet. He is just the – man I – want you to – marry.'

Darcia wanted to cry out that although she loved the Earl, there would never be any chance of his marrying her.

She was however silent, telling herself that nothing mattered except that her father should die happy.

There was a faint rustle near the door and she saw the *Marquise* come towards the bed to stand on the other side of it.

She stood looking down at Lord Rowley, then she crossed herself and went down on her knees beside him.

Her lips moved in prayer, then without speaking she rose to her feet and left Darcia alone once again with her father.

She must have sat in silence for ten or fifteen minutes until she felt the life-hold that he had on her hand beginning to relax.

'Papa!' she cried with a sudden urgency. 'Papa!'

His eye-lids fluttered very slightly. Then he said in a voice that was hardly audible: 'Goodbye – my Poppet–' and his hand fell away from hers.

For a moment Darcia could not believe it, could not acknowledge that her father was dead.

Then as she saw the Nun come quietly to the other side of him and she knew there was no hope, she went down on her knees to hide her face against him...

Darcia came out onto the terrace which overlooked the city.

Already the shadows were lengthening a little, growing purple beneath the cypress trees, and the heat was not so intense as it had been earlier in the day.

It had been very hot as her father was buried in the small Churchyard of the English Church, and the wreaths and flowers which had come from his friends and acquaintances had seemed to fill it.

The Funeral itself had been announced as being solely for the family, but beside Darcia and the *Marquise* there had been a whole crowd of people who she did not know, but who she felt had loved her father.

There were many beautiful women, men of his own age and younger who were prominent in the sporting world.

In addition, as if they considered themselves to be part of his family, representatives had come from all the great houses who had feted and admired Lord Rowley ever since he had first come to Italy.

It would have been impossible even if she had wanted to, to keep them away and Darcia could not help thinking that her father who had always been surrounded by his friends would have wanted them with him at the end.

Now it was all over and she had to face an empty life without him and … alone.

When the last carriage had driven away from the Villa and the servants had begun to tidy away the wine glasses and what was left of the food in the large white-pillared Dining-Room, the *Marquise* had gone up to her bedroom because she could no longer hide her tears.

Both she and Darcia had been very

controlled during the actual Funeral Service.

'Papa would hate me to cry in public,' Darcia told herself and she remembered too that tears had always annoyed him.

'Women use tears as a weapon to get their own way,' he had said to her more than once.

When she had been a very small child he had taken her on his knee to say:

'Laugh, my poppet, you look prettier when you laugh, and as a woman it's your duty to make other people laugh with you.'

During the Funeral Darcia felt almost as though her father was there, counting his friends, appreciating the magnificent floral tributes they had sent and laughing at those who believed that life ended with the grave.

How could anyone so vital, who enjoyed life so much, ever die?

At the same time it was going to be desperately hard to live without him.

'What shall I do, now that I am alone, Papa?' Darcia asked.

She wished as she had wished almost every moment since he had died, that she had had time to tell him of her problem and ask his advice.

'What would he have told me to do?' she wondered.

As always when she thought of the Earl it was an unbearable agony, physical as well as mental, so that she wondered how she could go on suffering and not die from the sheer pain of it.

She had moved a little way along the terrace so that she could no longer be seen from the windows of the house, and she now stood between two high cypress trees looking down at the vista below her.

Inevitably, because he was never far from her mind, she found herself thinking of the view the Earl had first shown her from the windows of his house.

It was then, although she did not know why, that the control she had placed upon herself since her father's death broke. She put her hands up to her eyes to stop the tears flooding down her cheeks and knew it was impossible.

Then as she stood shaking with the sheer intensity of her feelings she was suddenly not alone and two strong arms went around her.

She knew who it was, she knew who held her. But strangely it only made her unhappiness worse and she cried despairingly as a child might have done against his shoulder, her sobs shaking her whole body.

'It is all right, my darling, it is all right.'

She heard his voice, and thought she was dreaming, and yet for the moment she felt safe and secure, and his arms were the most comforting things she had ever known.

'Do not cry, my precious,' the Earl said, 'I cannot bear you to be so unhappy.'

'Papa … is … dead!'

Somehow through her tears Darcia spoke the words, feeling the Earl could not know what had happened.

'I know,' he said gently, 'and I shall miss him as you will. He was the happiest man I have ever known in my whole life. He gave everybody who knew him some of his inexhaustible joy of living.'

It was not at all what Darcia had expected the Earl to say about her father, and she raised her face wet with tears to look at him almost as if she wanted to assure herself that he was really there.

There was a kindness and a compassion in his eyes that she had never seen before and his arms tightened a little as he said very gently:

'Did you tell your father what we mean to each other?'

In the same uncanny way which had happened before, Darcia realised they were each aware of what each other was thinking and words were unnecessary.

It was difficult to speak so she only nodded her head.

'You told him I love you?' the Earl persisted.

'I ... said ... I ... I ... loved you,' Darcia corrected.

Then as if she remembered how hopeless her love was she hid her face against his shoulder again and asked in a muffled voice:

'Why ... are you ... here?'

'How could you have done anything so cruel as to leave without sending someone to tell me where you had gone, or why?'

There was silence for a moment, then Darcia said in a voice he could hardly hear:

'I ... I did not ... mean to see you ... again ... anyway.'

'I suspected that,' the Earl replied. 'In fact I was sure of it after you had left me that night and deliberately avoided saying when you would come to me as I wanted you to.'

Darcia felt herself tremble, but she managed to say with a bravery she had not known she possessed:

'I ... cannot do ... what you ... want me ... to do.'

'No, of course not,' the Earl agreed. 'It was

dreadfully wrong and extremely stupid of me to suggest anything of the sort in the first place.'

She felt him kiss her hair before he said:

'I have a lot of explaining to do, my precious one, but I know you must be tired after all you have been through today. Come and sit down and I will try to make you understand, although I do not deserve that you should.'

Because of the quiet way in which he spoke, but with a characteristic determination beneath it, Darcia found it impossible to go on crying.

She wiped her eyes and the Earl drew her gently across the grass to where there was a marble seat half-concealed by shrubs and trees.

They sat down and the Earl turning sideways to look at her as she lifted her eyes to his, her lashes still wet with tears, said, holding one of her hands in both of his:

'My Sweet! If you had only told me you had to leave England I would have come with you to look after you.'

'I ... I felt ... in a way ... that Fate had ... sent me away,' Darcia answered, 'since I knew that I could not ... live in the future ... with you as you ... wanted me to.'

'That is what I wanted to try to explain.'

'There is … no need,' she said quickly. '…I understand … and as I am not returning to … England … we will never … see each other … again.'

The Earl smiled.

'Do you really imagine I would allow you to walk out of my life and leave me alone?'

'I have to. It will be … difficult, but it would have been … easier if you had not come … h … here.'

As if she suddenly remembered that he should not have known who she was, she asked:

'How did you … find me?'

'I wondered when you would ask that question.'

The Earl looked down for a moment at her hand he held in his, then he said:

'It was after you had gone home that night and I felt inexpressibly happy at the thought of finishing my house with you to help me, then I suddenly realised what an utter fool I had been.'

Darcia glanced up at him enquiringly.

She did not understand what he was trying to say to her.

'I suppose,' the Earl went on, 'because it had been so firmly fixed in my mind that I was to marry Caroline the idea of marriage with anyone else never suggested itself to me. But I needed you and I knew you were everything that was right for my mind, my happiness, and for my house.'

Unexpectedly he bent his head and raising her hand kissed it.

'Then when I kissed you, my precious,' he said very quietly, 'I knew you were a part of me and the woman I had been looking for all my life.'

'I ... felt that ... too,' Darcia whispered.

'But I was too thick-headed to translate what I was feeling quite simply into the fact that I wanted you to be my wife.'

There was silence for a moment. Then Darcia said:

'It was my fault that you did not ... feel like that. I had wanted to see you again ever since you stayed at Rowley Park when I was only ten years old.'

She gave a little sob before she went on:

'But I thought when I came to England with strict instructions from ... Papa never to let anyone know that I was his daughter, that I could not bear to meet you as the *Comtesse* de Sauze. I wanted to make you ... aware of me in a very ... different manner.'

Her voice faltered for a moment before

she said:

'That was why I ... pretended to be a ... dealer and sold you things which I took from ... Rowley Park.'

'I knew that when I went there.'

'You ... went there?'

'When you did not turn up as I had hoped, I knew with the unaccountable perception that we have about each other, that I had lost you, so I went first to Rose Cottage.'

'Mrs Cosnett did not know who I was,' Darcia said quickly.

'No, but she told me quite inadvertently that the panelling which you sold me for the Breakfast Room had been intended for Rowley Park.'

'So you went there?'

'I went there, and it was not difficult to extract the information from the caretakers that the picture which had stood in the Silver Salon had only recently been removed. I could see the place on the wall where it had hung.'

There was silence for a moment. Then Darcia said:

'Did you ... guess then that I was ... Papa's daughter?'

'I did not have to guess,' the Earl answered. 'I saw a portrait of you in the Study.'

'That was … painted when I was … ten.'

'The same time that we first met. It is a very lovely picture, and I intend to hang if over the mantelpiece in our bedroom.'

He saw her eyes widen, but he said:

'I must finish telling you how I came here. I traced my cheques with which I had paid for the pictures and the panelling to a Bank where I learned an account had recently been opened in the name of the *Comtesse* de Sauze.'

'That was clever!' Darcia exclaimed.

'It was not difficult after that,' the Earl went on, 'to find that the *Comtesse* de Sauze was being talked about by everybody in the Social World, and her charm and her beauty were extolled quite ecstatically by almost every man I spoke to in my Club.'

He smiled as he said:

'When I learnt she had been staying with the *Marquise* de Beaulac, it only remained for me to find out where they had gone.'

'I cannot believe it was Mr Curtis who told you!' Darcia exclaimed.

'I had to bully him a little,' the Earl admitted, 'especially as I recognised him as the servant of Mr Quincey!'

'He must have been astonished to see you.'

'He was more discomfited than astonished,' the Earl answered. 'He was also surprised that I knew that you were Lord Rowley's daughter, and when I threatened to interrogate every member of the staff unless he told me where you had gone, he finally gave me your address.'

'So ... you are ... here,' Darcia said in a very small voice.

'I am here, and I only wish it could have been a few days sooner, so that I could have told your father that I would look after you and how happy I would make you.'

He felt Darcia's fingers stiffen in his and he said very quietly:

'We *will* be happy, my darling, and our children, as you so rightly anticipated, will doubtless make the house too small, and we shall have to build another wing.'

He saw the radiance which seemed to light Darcia's face. Then she said quickly:

'You ... cannot ... marry me.'

'Why not?'

'Because ... as Papa said when he sent me to ... England ... as the *Comtesse* de Sauze, nobody ... important could marry me ... because of his ... reputation.'

'I do not know whether I am important or not,' the Earl replied, 'but I have every intention of marrying you.'

'N ... no, you must not do ... that.'

'Why not?'

'Because everything about you is so ... so perfect.'

There was a little pause. Then she said in a voice he could hardly hear:

'It was because I wanted our ... love to be ... perfect that I knew I could not ... live with you ... as you suggested.'

'In that you were absolutely and completely right. But as you have said, my darling, I want perfection, and that is what I have found in you.'

'B ... but ... Papa...'

'Your father, because he loved you was being over-protective, over-apprehensive and it is what I too will be in the future.'

He put his arm around her as he spoke and pulled her close to him.

'Personally,' he went on, 'I do not care a damn what anybody says except that it might upset you. We will be married quietly under your present name, which is entirely legal, and the name you are known by in one society.'

He pulled her closer to him as he continued:

'Then when nobody will argue, at least

openly, with me about my wife, everyone in the world as far as I am concerned can know who your father was. The majority, like myself, will remember him as a great sports-man.'

'What you are saying ... cannot be ... true!'

Then she was crying again, crying tears of sheer happiness because the Earl was holding her close and she was no longer frightened of the future.

'I love ... you! I love ... you!' she sobbed. 'I never thought ... I never ... dreamed ... you would ever feel like this ... about me...'

'But I do,' the Earl said, 'and since I cannot live without you, you have to start thinking of me.'

'I do ... that anyway. You ... fill my whole world and then sky, and there is ... no-one else but ... you.'

She turned her face up to his and he looked down at her very tenderly.

'I love you!' he said, 'and I know now I have never been in love before, and this is a perfection I had no idea existed.'

As he spoke his lips were on hers and as he kissed her in what Darcia knew was very different from the way in which he had kissed her before.

His lips were demanding, tender and possessive but gentle. The violence had gone, and yet because he was touching her, because she was close against him the rapture was even more intense, more wonderful than it had been before.

She could feel the glory of it sweeping up through her body evoking the fire that had seemed to consume them both as if they were in the heat of the sun.

At the same time there was something else.

It was what she had known had been in her love, but thought never to find in his.

It was the ecstasy of the Divine, the spiritual glory that she knew came from God.

'I love you ... I love ... you!' she tried to say.

But the Earl was holding her closer and still closer to him and was kissing her in a way which told her because she could read his thoughts that despite his self-assurance he had been desperately afraid that he had lost her and would never find her again.

'You are mine!' he cried. 'Mine completely and absolutely! You will never leave me again. This is what I have always wanted. This is why I built my house, to make a home that would be filled with love, the love, my darling, that only you can give me.'

'You are … sure? Sure that you … really want me?'

It was like waking from a nightmare to have him saying things she had thought never to hear.

'It will take me the whole of our lives to tell you how much I love you,' the Earl said, 'and, my precious, there is much for us to do together, things I could never do with any other woman because they would not understand.'

Darcia knew that was true and she thought, strange though it seemed, that only the life she had lived with her eccentric, unpredictable, adorable father would have made it possible for her to understand the Earl and be able to give him the companionship that would make their marriage perfect.

Fate had certainly worked in strange and diverse ways to bring them what they needed.

Now the plan was complete, and they were together. Like the Earl's house there were only a few finishing touches to make it complete.

Looking down at her the Earl thought he

had never seen anyone look so happy, so radiant in a manner that was unearthly and almost inhuman.

'I love you, Darcia!' he said, 'and I want to go on saying so over and over again until I convince you that we are one person and without each other there is no happiness for either of us.'

'That is what I feel,' Darcia answered, 'although I could not ... believe that you would ... feel the same.'

'I begged you to trust me and in future remember that I always get my own way.'

He smiled in a manner which she thought was irresistible as he went on:

'I have been looking for perfection, I have worked for it, and now in marrying you I shall achieve it.'

He gave a little laugh and added:

'That sounds conceited, my precious, but if it is, then I am prepared to be the most conceited man in the world because I shall be your husband, and you will be my wife.'

Because of the way he spoke Darcia laughed too.

'That is what I want to hear,' the Earl said tenderly, 'and that is what I cannot live without – your laughter, and the joy you bring to everything you do which makes you very much your father's daughter.'

'Papa admired you ... even when you were young ... for the way you ... rode,' Darcia said with a little break in her voice.

'I know that he would want me to look after you,' the Earl replied, 'and we will call our first son after him.'

Darcia gave a little inarticulate murmur and hid her face against his shoulder.

'Am I making you shy, my darling one?' the Earl asked. 'There is no need. We have talked about so many things together and it was you who told me that my house needed a family and now it is you who must provide it.'

'I have ... always wanted to ... have your ... children,' Darcia said in a whisper.

'I think, my lovely one, we should get married first,' the Earl teased, 'and as I have no intention of waiting for you one moment longer than I need to, we will be married tomorrow!'

'So soon?' Darcia was about to say, then checked herself.

She knew from this moment on she was prepared to leave herself and her future in the Earl's hands.

She belonged to him and it was for him to do what he wished, knowing only too well it was her wish too.

Her eyes were shining, and there was a smile on her lips as she stretched up her arm to pull his head down to hers.

'Tomorrow seems … a long time … away,' she said very softly.

She was unable to say any more for he was kissing her passionately, compellingly.

At the same time the tenderness was still there and she knew the love he had for her was what she wanted – both physical and spiritual.

Real love which in itself is the perfection of God.

The publishers hope that this book has given you enjoyable reading. Large Print Books are especially designed to be as easy to see and hold as possible. If you wish a complete list of our books please ask at your local library or write directly to:

Magna Large Print Books
Magna House, Long Preston,
Skipton, North Yorkshire.
BD23 4ND

This Large Print Book, for people
who cannot read normal print,
is published under the auspices of

THE ULVERSCROFT FOUNDATION